ADAM'S APPLE

by
Kira Kenley

To Anne, creative friend and kindred spirit.

'Let go or be dragged.'
Zen Proverb

'Ah walked in the footsteps of ma father. Ah got a girl knocked up and then Ah ran. Just like him. Ja, Ah proved ma mother's point. The apple does not fall far from the tree.'
Denzel Anderson

Contents

SID I

Being dead is not an easy thing – at least, it hasn't been for me. Dying was pretty straight forward. All I had to do was let go of my physical form, which was a welcome release considering that my throat had just been cut open and I was bleeding all over myself. Of course, it did mean leaving Holly. But right in that moment, it was fear more than love that gripped me, so I happily stepped away from my body, and the pain and anxiety I felt when Carl stabbed me ebbed away while the sea washed the Ibizan shore close by. The actual stabbing had been quick. However, it was the feeling afterwards that was really terrifying – the panic that set in when I knew I was fatally wounded and there was no going back. In a split second my life was pulled away from me, my survival no longer an option, and every cell of my body relayed that message in unison like a choir delivering a final crescendo.

Carl joined me on this side of the fence soon after. An assisted drug overdose meant that he was left, like me, walking on the periphery. At first it was all very entertaining, watching and discovering the things I had no idea about when I was alive. But then as this new reality settled with me, it became less interesting. Unlike me, Carl moved on very quickly. He was there one minute and then he was gone, like a hologram. But me, I'm still here. I haven't had to make a deal with God or any such deity. If there is a god of some sort, we have yet to meet.

When I first crossed over there was a woman here – the mother I never had but would imagine. Her name was Peggy, just a couple of characters different from Penny, my own mother's name. Peggy told me the things that I couldn't quite process in those first surreal moments when

I died, and she had helped me in the earlier stages to readjust. I discovered I already knew everything, but I needed someone to help me piece it all together. She was the loveliest woman I might ever have met – very like Eileen Brady, my best friend Dave's mother. I had always envied him his family. Peggy listened and held me a lot, something I hadn't experienced much when I was alive. And then one day she passed through as I watched in awe – very different to Carl's prompt departure. It was like nothing I'd ever seen before; to attempt to find words to explain the cycle of life would be pointless, so I won't. It is quite simply indescribable and demonstrates that no matter what happens in real life we are all made of the same stuff – energy! That's all we are – free at the deepest level, no matter what our minds and bodies might have us believe.

As Peggy explained, everything depends on order. I can see it all now, and am privy to information that lets me see that everything in this life happens for a reason, a reason that is always the same: so that the next thing can happen. It's that simple. Really. Life is relentless, and it's much easier for us if we just go with its flow. Dying has taught me that, more than living ever did. I see now that life is constantly moving; only in death does everything stop.

The thing that's been the hardest to adapt to is how the mind and the astral body are one and the same thing. So when I think about something without knowing that I am merely thinking, I'm right back there as if it's happening again. Like when I recall my own death: I'm back on the beach feeling it all again, re-experiencing each terrifying moment. And every time I crash from one reality into another my stomach feels like it's turning itself inside out. I feel nauseous, which is an odd experience now that throwing up is no longer an option.

When I ponder my future I go there too, and can see a version of it in vivid colour, although the future is a bit harder to pin down as it hasn't happened yet – I have no reference point and it doesn't always make sense. And when I think of a person I end up in their present, a witness to the events happening in their lives in the here and now, in real time as Jack Bauer liked to say at the beginning of the TV series 24. The experience is kind of like I'm scanning through the channels on a virtual afterlife TV.

In the time since my death, my ability to travel via my thoughts into the present has meant that I've seen a lot more of my father than I ever did when I was alive. Bill, the love of his life, has travelled from New York to be with him. It makes me happy for him, but sad for me – happy that he has finally stopped punishing himself for his part in my mother's suicide, but sad because I will never have the chance to have a relationship like that with Holly. That is the most tragic thing about my death. The love I'd dreamed of experiencing for such a long time had happened, but then I went and got myself killed. It's typical Sid Harris behaviour.

Deep down I knew my death was coming. I had this dread that my new-found happiness would be taken away. And then it was. That was what sent me back to see my father in London not long after I ran away to Ibiza. We had our first ever conversation about Penny's death, and he had given me her suicide note to read, wanting me to know his secret but not able to tell me himself. Finding out my father was gay came as a total shock, although it was obvious once I knew, and it explained so much about his behaviour while I was growing up. I told him I loved him – the one and only time I ever did – but he never said it back. He couldn't. And now I am watching an altered Tim

Harris struggle to have the kind of relationship we could never have had with Denzel, my friend and brother.

The fact that I met and became friends with my half-brother is something I only discovered after I'd died. It was a shock, but it seemed obvious once I knew, much like when I learned that my father was gay. One of the reasons Denzel and I became such good friends was this sense of closeness I had felt but couldn't put my finger on back then. Now I know that that is what it feels like to have a brother – someone who came from the same place you did. My death brought this fact to light, and my father stumbled across his firstborn son as he collected the pieces of me that I had left in Ibiza. It changed everything for both of them.

The Denzel Anderson that walks the earth these days is nothing like the lunatic I first encountered in Ibiza. He is married to Alice, his childhood sweetheart, and they are expecting their first baby, a niece or nephew for me and a grandchild for Tim Harris. For a time everything has been charmed, but now Denzel has a feeling of dread similar to what I felt back in Ibiza, a feeling that his happiness might all be about to end. And just as my fear was justified back then, so is his, for I have seen it first-hand. My brother's past is coming to get him, and Holly is in danger too.

I think of her now and let the thought take me to her side. I watch her as she sits with Raphael in Paris. My stomach hurls, and not just because of the sudden change of location – I hate seeing her with someone else. I wish I didn't; I wish that I was content for her to be happy without me. But the truth is I want to be with her and I hate watching this. I'm jealous, and it hurts me in death as much as it would in life. That's another thing I have learned about death: I am still the same person with the same habits. Those don't alter when we die. What we are in life comes with us.

My family is being watched like prey, and the person watching them is damaged and filled with hatred. As his pain grows it moves him further into the darkness, and I am scared about what he might do. He is my nephew, a child born from a secret that is coming to topple my brother's happiness. His name is Adam and he seeks revenge. He is hovering nearby the ones I love. When I am around him I can feel his festering rage and it intensifies my fear. I have no idea what I can do to stop him, and now that Peggy is gone, there is no one here I can ask.

Bewildered, I watch with a heavy heart as the person who means the most to me in life and death walks straight into the flames.

1
Stagnant In Paris

Alors, Denzel is having a baby while I, Holly Du Plessis, am still in mourning, like a forgotten widow whose place in the world is defined solely by her dead loved one. *La vie, c'est injuste*!

I look at the message on my screen, which tells me that life goes on, that love continues for others. But for me? Non. I really want to be happy for Denzel. I had seen him in Ibiza in a great state of misery and watched his decline. His second chance at life, at love, should make me feel happy. But I am afraid it does not. I only feel resentful. Papa says that bitterness kills your heart, that it takes root inside and squeezes all the love out of you. He is right, for these days my heart feels empty and cold. All the love has left.

Sid Harris.

I wonder why it was that you came into my life. Was it so that I would know how it feels to be in love? So I would know what it feels like to really and truly care for someone and for them to love me back? To know the great comfort and assurance that is in that feeling? Life suddenly feels sweet. And safe. You begin to believe in love, something you once thought was foolish and made up by those who could not bear to live with reality. And then love leaves. It is gone, just like that. One day you and I were making plans for the future and the next you were taken away from me. Although it is over a year since you left this world, I still feel your loss, almost more intently now. And then this email from Denzel, after almost six months of silence, to say that he had been thinking of me as we passed through the anniversary of your death, and telling me that he is bringing a new life into the world. He wants me to know that he and his wife, Alice, have set about making another person for this world, as if it might compensate for your absence. Absurd! But I suppose love has made him sentimental.

It seems that Denzel and Alice married in London shortly after I last saw him in Paris. He had invited me to their wedding and sounded shocked that I would not come. But for me, it seemed like the worst thing to have to do, to sit and watch two people declare that they would spend a life together when the one person I would have liked to spend my life with is dead and has taken my happiness with him. Denzel had found his Alice, the great love of his youth who he had left back in South Africa. He had found her, still living and breathing. He told me all about it. And as I bore witness to his story, the bitterness that had set in the morning he told me of Sid's death took deeper root. It had been easy to be a friend to him when he was suffering like me. But now it is different, not so easy.

Denzel thought I might blame him and I told him I didn't. Sid, my English boy, newly in my life, had died saving him, his friend, who turned out to be his brother. *Incroyable*! But the truth was more complex, as it always is. Simple is the story we make up when the truth is too hard. I did not blame Denzel then, but now I am angry and resentful of everyone. It is all over me. I see it in my behaviour and in my work, which has become dark, like my father's. Gone is the light of Ibiza. Gone is my love of colour. The pictures I work on now are clouded in greys and blacks, and speak of fear and loss and death. Love is absent.

The world in which I live tastes sour and my experiences do little to sweeten it, as they did before. I can remember when I was intoxicated with life, but now everything is flat, like champagne that has been opened prematurely, its fizz dying out in the bottle. Perhaps I need a change of surroundings. Again the thought that has been plaguing me pushes to the front of my mind: the urge to go to London, to the homeland of Sid Harris, to be close to him again. Before Sid I was different. I said I was a realist while others proclaimed me to be a free spirit. I thought it was madness to wish to be tied to one person when there were so many on the planet. We were not designed to be faithful to only one; otherwise why did we feel attracted to so many? But then I met Sid and my feelings changed. I had been quite shocked when this oddly beautiful boy had come and touched me deeply, broke me open like an egg. How cruel that I am left open, exposed, without him; a broken egg unable to return to my shell, yet unable to move forward. Life is cruel. Or perhaps it is love that is cruel. Love is only for the birds, Papa says.

I look out of the lounge window at the best view in all of Paris and prepare to leave it.

'*Bonjour, chérie!*'

Raphael, my lover and oldest friend, comes to join me. We have fallen together again. He says he loves me and that he always will, no matter what. I pity him the cross he bears, for I will never love him – not like he wants me to. It is the truth. I could lie, say I might grow to love him and we'd live happily ever after, but it will not happen. I think he knows this too, deep down. But Raphael Conti is from a rich and powerful family, used to getting what they want, and the idea that he cannot have what he wants makes him stubborn, reluctant to give up.

He is not alone in his wish for us to be together, for Papa has, on many occasions, expressed a wish to see me with Raphael. Papa wants me settled and with a family, unlike him who never married. Hypocrite! But I love him dearly despite his contrary behaviour. Sid had no qualities in common with Papa, and that was probably why Sid captured my heart, although they say that girls fall for men like their fathers. There is much I did not get to know about Sid in the real world, but my portraits of him showed me much of his inner world. It all pours out in the brushstrokes, revealing that which is right there in front of the eyes but which we become blind to. Yes, Sid Harris was a completely different fish to the man who raised me.

I say good morning to Raphael. He asks me how I am and if I am hungry. I let him cook us some eggs. He is the best cook I know, unlike me. Pia was an amazing cook too. But now she is no longer in my life. Remembering her makes me sad. Pia was the reason I was in Ibiza. We met at university and had been lovers for a time – my only time with a woman. It was enough to let me know it was men I craved; not even an incredibly beautiful girl like Pia could compete with my primal need for the opposite sex. We became friends afterwards, my only friendship with another woman other than Bebe, my mother in everything but blood (the woman who gave birth to me was not worthy of that title; she had been a gold-digging bitch who had tried to trap my father and left as soon as he had tightened his purse strings). Pia was the only girlfriend I felt completely at ease with. There was no competitiveness; just deep respect and care. But then she had got involved with Marco and her drug habit took over and our friendship ended.

'Where are you?' Raphael asks me in English and it takes me by surprise. Usually we speak in French.

'I am remembering Pia,' I say in English.

'Still no contact?'

I shake my head.

'I am worried about you,' Raphael says as we share a cigarette after our eggs.

I do not answer.

'I have never seen you like this – ever, in all our years together. It is as if a part of life has left you.'

'A part of life *has* left me. I lost someone I loved very much,' I tell him.

He looks uncomfortable. That is why I do not speak to him of Sid. He had been extremely hurt by the whole affair, recognising the presence of something important in my relationship with Sid that has always been absent in our relationship.

'But you hardly knew him!' he says.

I flare up and instinctively revert to French. 'You do not understand, Raphael. I loved him! It does not take any time to fall in love. You claim to know all about love yet you do not know this thing!' The words jump out of my mouth and rain down on him. 'I am sorry, Raphael.'

I mean it and he knows I mean it. He nods.

'I know this has been going on for a long time,' I say, 'but I have an idea.'

He lights up another cigarette and hands it to me. I take a drag. Then I tell him I want to take a little trip. Do I want him to come with me is his next question, of course. I shake my head. I will go to London with the spirit of Sid inside of me, where it dwells these days. I will go to see if perhaps the turn of events that saw Denzel miraculously turn his life around might help me too. Yes, I will move, for here in Paris I am starting to die, and if this bitterness gets any bigger it will swallow me whole.

'*Quand*?' Raphael asks.

'*Aujourd'hui*,' I reply. This is a state of emergency, I think to myself.

'Why do you punish me, Holly?' he asks me in English.

'*Je ne sais pas*,' I reply.

It is the truth.

2

London: The Beginning

The key finds its way into the lock, and a moment later I am inside Papa's London apartment. It is very beautiful, with the most wonderful view. Papa finds places with great views everywhere he chooses to live, and London is no exception. I open the velvet curtains and look out at Tower Bridge. Papa has painted this bridge many times, and perhaps I might follow in his footsteps. But it will depend on what comes when I begin to work.

Like all Du Plessis homes, there is a huge studio, a place for Papa and me to paint. I am longing to paint in my new surroundings. My hands are itchy for my paint brushes. I cannot go far these days without creating something. I need to create, to make something, to have something to show for my life in which I feel lost. It grounds me. At least when I paint I leave physical evidence that, regardless of how dead I feel inside, something about me is still alive.

I think about Raphael and his reaction to my announcement about losing someone I loved very much. He has a vested interest in how I deal with Sid's loss and wishes I could find a way that included him. But he cannot be objective about my life, any more than I can. I left him in a bad place in Paris, but that is nothing unusual. I am forever leaving him in bad places. My treatment of Raphael in the past has been unfair to him, I know this, but the truth is, I need him to need me. It is something that keeps me strong and makes me feel like I am not alone. He claims that he will always be there for me, waiting for me to change my mind. If only it were so simple! I am trapped in this vortex and it hits me hard that my desire for Sid may never leave me. After all, it has been more than a year since he went and I still feel the same.

And here I am in his homeland. But for what? To torture myself further in the hope that the awful longing will leave me? Or did I think it might be possible to meet someone else? Perhaps if I was near Denzel and his new-found happiness it might rub off on me. I am not sure of my motives or what has really driven me here, but here I am and now I must make the most of it, especially as I have upset Raphael again. But that is what he has come to expect of me. It is what I am best at doing – hurting him and making him suffer and wishing he had never set eyes on me. Although he claims to love me, I am not sure if that is what it really is, for it makes neither of us happy. Unlike Sid and I. Our love made us hopeful and stronger; it brought us together. But what do I know! It was so long ago and for such a short time. Here one minute and then gone. The bitterness shows itself again and I pray that painting is the answer, that creating something on canvas will diminish what is growing inside my heart and twisting everything.

I am jealous. It is a new emotion that I knew little of before Sid's death. All around me I see love. It is as if every couple in the world is finding their way towards me. And all the time I am full of hatred, wishing that I had what they have, and feeling all alone.

I have come here to see Denzel, and his Alice too. I'm not sure why. Do I feel safer as an onlooker in love? Or am I looking to be redeemed somehow? To change? To be near love in the hope that it will melt my freezing heart?

I remember when Denzel and I first met. He was a friend of Marco's, Pia's ape of a boyfriend, but different from the usual types that Marco hung around with.

Initially I had found him unsettlingly attractive. Raw and wild. I had wanted to paint him and then to sleep with him, as I did most of the models I worked with once the art was completed. However, when I began working with Denzel I saw only his pain and troubles. It was too much and I backed away, afraid of what might happen to me if I let him into my body. I believe we wear whoever we sleep with – take a piece of them with us and carry it through our lives – so it is wise to select well to ensure you carry with you those who will serve you best. Papa has told me it is quite different for men. Men can cast it away, forget us forever. But we keep them close. So all the people I have had sex with are inside me, but Sid takes centre stage. He is the only one I loved.

For a time after Sid died I would speak to him, but he remained silent. My pleas for him to comfort me were left unanswered, confirming for me that after we die there is nothing. If there were something after death, he would have come back to help me fill the awful black hole he left. Nor has time healed the wound, as the sentimental writers promise. I still feel it as if it were yesterday. I have cleaned myself up, thrown myself into my work, gone back to Raphael, but none of it has helped. I am still empty. Lost. Alone. I feel nothing of Sid around me because he is gone. Dead. And I am still here. Without him.

It is close to madness, and I would probably be in danger of going over the edge if it were not for my art. It is always there to take my mind off the emptiness. And now the newness in my surroundings will help. I will throw myself head first into learning all the ways of this London life and begin again. I'll start over again, a bit like Sid did when he came to Ibiza.

Perhaps I can find someone new, someone who will kiss it all away and make it better. Surely there is someone else out there for me. Why would Sid have been sent to open up my heart if there was no one else for me to love?

But what if there is not? Papa has spent most of his life alone. I had not seen that as a problem. I had even thought that it might be the best way of life for me too. But then I met Sid Harris and felt how it was to be with someone I loved, and now it is painful to be without. I hate this want inside of me, and sometimes I hate you, Sid Harris, for being the cause of this unhappiness. But always, when the hate fades, I go back to missing you. And loving you.

The universe hates a vacuum, Papa says, and I believe him. Just as the canvas does not stay blank for long, neither will I. While I am here I will start again. I will paint afresh and see this vibrant city like I have never seen it before. And I will watch for the possibility of love, returning to me in another form, as I look for inspiration.

I will take the next few days to look around and let it reveal itself to me. First the eye sees, and then the blank canvas becomes filled with what it has seen. I will watch London, my subject, and see what it gives me. In Ibiza, people's faces had jumped out at me begging for me to paint them, and one of those faces had been sent to love me.

Sid Harris. Again he is back. His face. His eyes. His heart drawing me close.

The memory of Sid stays with me and I feel alone. I need some kind of connection. I have it in this city. Denzel Anderson is the person who connects me to my love and has proved himself a friend since Sid left.

I hit the call button and after only a few rings he answers.

'Holly! How goes it?'

'I am here, Denzel!'

'Ja, and Ah am here.'

'No, I mean I am here in your here.'

'You're in London?'

'*Oui!*'

'Alice, Holly is in London!'

Silence.

'Come see us,' says Denzel.

'Of course! Soon.'

'Na. Now. What are you doing now?'

'Nothing.'

'Well then, come here.'

'Okay.'

'Alice says come for supper. Okay?'

'Yes, okay. Supper is dinner, *oui*?'

'Ja. Grab a pen and I'll tell you where to go. It's good to hear your voice, Holly.'

'Yours too, Denzel.'

And it really is. It makes me feel better than I have felt in the longest time.

3

A Dinner Date

'It's lovely to meet you Holly,' says a very pregnant-looking Alice, extending her hand.

She is beautiful. Elegant, and not at all the kind of woman I would have put Denzel Anderson with. Tame. I would have imagined he'd want wild. This woman is most definitely not wild. Of course, this is a different Denzel Anderson to the one I had known in Ibiza. Very different. But his wildness is still there underneath; untameable. I sense it.

'You are very pregnant,' I say.

'Yes.' She smiles at me, but I don't believe her smile.

She scrutinises me, assessing my connection to her husband, and seems to come to the conclusion that she does not like me or our connection. Her jealousy is obvious to me, and I wonder if it is to her husband. It is a shame as it will make it hard for me to become fond of her; I think I need to grow fond of her for all of our sakes.

'Ma beautiful pregnant wife,' Denzel gushes, smiling so much that his face looks like it might burst open. He is in love. Mon Dieu, he is in love! It is as if he has just been rolled in the stuff.

'Please sit down, Holly,' Alice says, too busy taking me in to notice how her husband is watching her.

I want to shake her until she stops taking such things for granted. I let it run through my mind, how it would have been if Sid and I had got this chance; how he would look at me as I carried his child. Yes, I feel your jealousy, Alice, but I have a reason to feel it. You do not. Your love is living. Your stupidity makes you undeserving of what you have.

She ushers me into a living room where a table is set for dinner. The table is set for five and I wonder who the other two will be.

'So, Holly, tell me what's happening. Why are you here in London?' Denzel asks.

'I decided to come and stay for a while. To paint.'

'That's great,' he says and he looks genuinely happy. 'It will be good to have you around.'

Alice says nothing. I notice, but he is oblivious to her unrest. Sometimes men do not see what is right in front of them. *Incroyable*!

'I'll get on with dinner,' Alice says lightly, but there is still a frostiness there. She leaves us.

'You want a drink, Holly?' Denzel asks.

'Wine would be good, please,' I reply.

'You are no longer on the wagon?' he says.

'No.'

He pours two glasses of wine.

'You neither?'

'Na. But alcohol was never the problem. Cocaine was the one in danger of detonating me. Ja, for sure.'

'Cheers, Holly.'

'Cheers, Denzel. Your wife – she is very beautiful,' I say.

'Ja, she is.'

'And you will soon be a father. Amazing.'

'Ja. Speaking of fathers, mine is joining us tonight.'

'Oh! I will meet Tim Harris?'

'Ja. It seems fitting, don't you think?'

'I suppose,' I reply.

'Really, how are you, Holly?' I can hear real concern in his voice.

'Not good. That is why I am here. I cannot forget and somehow I thought coming here, somewhere new but somewhere that is full of him, might help me. It is crazy?'

'Na. Ah think Ah understand, actually. It helped me to come here and live in his home. Ah stayed in his room downstairs until Alice and I moved into this apartment six months ago.'

'Of course, this is Sid's home! I forgot somehow.'

It hits me and with it a wave of resentment. If things had been different it could have been Sid and me living here, with his father close by.

The door bell sounds. Alice calls out that she will get it and a few minutes later I hear the voice of Sid's father. It strikes me as being a lot like Sid's. He comes through the door, but physically I see only Denzel.

'Holly, it is lovely to meet you,' Tim says and smiles at me. A half-smile. Sid. Sid. Sid.

'Yes, and you Monsieur Harris,' I reply, surprising myself that I want to make an impression.

'Tim, please.'

'And I'm Bill, Tim's partner.' A handsome man pops out from behind Tim. 'Lovely to meet you,' he says and takes my hand firmly. He moves like he is no stranger to the stage.

'Good timing,' Alice announces. 'The food is just ready.'

'Great!' Bill says. 'I'm famished. Where shall we sit, Alice?'

Alice seats us at her table like we are part of the table settings. She is in control. I am placed at the table's edge between Bill and Tim, far away from her and Denzel. This woman really feels threatened by me, and I wonder what fuels her insecurity. Is it something she senses from me or from Denzel? Wherever it emanates from, the charge in this room fascinates me.

We sit down and wait while Denzel goes to help in the kitchen.

'So, Holly, what brings you to London?' Bill asks.

'I have come to get out of Paris for a while.'

'But why would anyone want to get out of Paris?'

'It is time. I've been there a lot of years. I feel like a change is necessary.'

'Of course! I moved back from New York recently after a lifetime away. New York was great but it wasn't home. Is Paris home?'

'Most certainly. I just needed a change,' I repeat.

Denzel and Alice serve the food and then join us.

'You're okay for a drink, Holly?' Denzel asks.

'Yes, thank you.'

'Where are you staying?' Alice asks. Her first question, establishing territory.

'Tower Bridge. My papa has an apartment there.'

'Not far away, and another nice part of town,' Bill says.

'Yes,' I reply.

'This food is delicious, Alice,' Bill comments.

'Thank you,' says Alice, beaming.

'What have you seasoned the chicken with? Tarragon, chives and something else, I think.'

'You have an exceptional palate, Bill. Tarragon, chives and fresh lemon. It makes the meat so tender.'

'Ah yes! And it tastes great. You like to cook, Holly?'

'No. It is not something I enjoy.'

'What do you enjoy?' Bill asks. I find myself warming to this man very quickly. He is interested and it feels genuine. Yes, I like him very much.

'Painting, dancing, and eating food rather than making it,' I reply simply.

'Holly is an amazing artist,' Denzel cuts in.

'Now I remember!' Bill announces. 'Denzel went to your exhibition in Paris at the beginning of the year.'

I nod my head.

'You painted some very beautiful pictures of my son,' Tim says. It is the first thing he has said since we sat down. I look at him, meeting his eyes and feeling something of Sid.

'I saw them online,' he adds. 'If I'd been brave enough I'd have gone to the show.'

'Thank you,' I say. 'I have listened to your music, Tim. It is very beautiful.'

'I merely extract it from the ether.'

'As carefully as you can and in the hope that you do it justice,' I finish and he smiles.

'Precisely.'

A moment passes between us.

'I can see why Sid fell in love with you, Holly,' he says.

The sound of smashing glass shatters our moment.

'God, I'm sorry,' Alice says, and all attention is back on her where I think she likes it to be.

'I am so clumsy these days. Pregnancy!' she says and smiles.

'It is your first baby, Alice?' I ask and she looks sharply at me.

'Yes.'

'When is it due?'

'November,' she replies.

'Shame it's not going to be a New Year's baby like me. There's always a party,' Bill says.

'Na,' Denzel cuts in. 'What if he is like his anti-social father and doesn't want to celebrate at all. Then what?'

'He will be a right little social animal if his grandpa Bill has anything to do with it! When is your birthday, Holly?'

'January third.'

'Here's to January babies,' he says and raises his glass.

'And March ones,' Denzel cuts in. 'Alice is the sixth and Ah'm the ninth. We were born only three days apart.'

'And what about you, Tim? When is your birthday?' I ask.

'It's today,' he says.

'Na!' Denzel says.

'I prefer not to celebrate,' Tim says, and Bill rests his hand on Tim's. It is done so tenderly that it makes me want to cry.

I excuse myself after establishing where the toilet is. I make it there and barely get the door locked before I begin to sob into my hands. I am sad, but mostly I feel incredibly resentful and bitter, and I think again about what Papa said about bitterness and what it does to a heart. His words are true because I feel it twist inside mine now. I hope it will pass through me as I cry.

On my way back to the dining room, I find the front door slightly open and hear someone coughing outside. A smoker. I open the door expecting to see Denzel, but instead I find Bill.

'Having a timeout,' he explains and passes the packet my way.

I take one and light up, thinking of Sid.

'You've been crying,' he says.

'Yes. It upset me, the conversation – realising I do not know when Sid's birthday is. Imagine!'

'My darling girl, these Harris boys are not normal. You must have worked that one out!' He winks and it makes me smile.

'How long have you and Tim been together?' I ask.

'Off and on all our lives. He contacted me after Sid passed away and here we are.'

'You knew Sid?'

'Yes, I did. But not very well, I'm afraid. It was a difficult situation.'

'Why?' I can guess the answer, but I would prefer to know.

'Well, Tim was married to Sid's mother so …'

'Ahhh, you were having an affair.'

'Quite.'

'I see how you would not have been the best of friends, then.'

He smiles. 'How long were you and Sid together?' he asks.

'We met in Ibiza just before he died.'

'I am so sorry,' he says.

I nod my head. 'I miss him all the time. It is strange because I did not know him so long and was fine before, but now I am a mess. How is this possible?'

'I am sorry, my dear girl, but that is love. You loved him and it never disappears.'

'You never forgot Tim?'

'No. I didn't even try. I knew it was pointless. Don't get me wrong – it's not that there wasn't anyone else. There was, and there will be for you, I'm sure. But I just didn't try to look for what I'd had with Tim. I didn't expect it from anyone else.'

'And then you found Tim again.'

'Yes. I'm sorry, Holly. I'm probably saying all the wrong things.'

'No, actually you are telling the truth and I appreciate that. I hate when people lie to me. It is so obvious when people lie. Non?'

He nods. 'You and Denzel appear very close,' he says eventually.

'Yes. I think we helped each other after Sid died. But I am not so sure any more, now he is with Alice and the baby is coming. His mind is with them, as it should be. I don't know why I came here actually. It seemed like a good idea, but now that I am here and sitting in the middle of a family that has no place for me, it feels wrong.

I don't belong and I feel resentful of you all. It feels really horrible. Mon Dieu! Why am I spilling all of this to you? I am sorry!'

'Please don't be. Complete strangers are the best people to talk to.'

'But somehow you do not feel like a complete stranger!'

'And that, my dear, is the rock upon which I have perished all my life.' He gives me a mischievous smile and it makes me laugh.

This is how Denzel finds us, laughing like two old friends. 'Ah might have known you'd be having a sneaky fag,' he says to Bill.

'You have still quit?' I ask.

'Ja! And it's just as well, with the baby coming.'

'I cannot believe the change in you, Denzel. You should have seen him in Ibiza,' I say to Bill. 'Like a wild animal on the loose.'

'I can well believe that,' Bill replies and nods his head.

'Ja,' Denzel says and flashes his wicked smile. 'Ah remember him well. But Ah prefer the boet Ah see in the mirror these days, for sure. The same old same old, but with less of the darkness.'

I recall the painting I did of him and as if he has read my mind he begins to speak about it.

'Holly once painted ma picture in Ibiza. It was not a vision for the faint-hearted, for sure. Ah looked like something out of Dante's Inferno.'

'Well, if that's the case I'm glad I met you when you'd left your former self behind,' Bill says and stubs out his cigarette. 'I should go back and check that your father isn't commandeering the conversation like he usually does … Not!' He winks before disappearing inside.

'He is great!' I say.

'Ja, he is,' Denzel replies. 'Have you been crying?'

'Sorry, Denzel! I am in a state and I came here to see if I could shift it. But, you know, it is hard to be around you like this.'

'Na, Ah should be the one saying sorry! It can't be easy coming to Sid's home and Ah probably shouldn't have invited Tim tonight. That was stupid of me, ja?'

'Non, that is not what I am talking about. It is you – you and Alice – seeing you in love and happy and expecting a baby. I am really resentful because I wish it were Sid here with me carrying his child. I am sorry, but that is how I feel. Maybe it would be best if I don't see you for a while.'

'Ah don't think that is the answer. Ah'll come see you tomorrow, just you and me, and we can forget about all of this and just concentrate on what's happening for you. Ja?'

He says it so matter-of-factly that it makes me laugh.

'Why are you laughing?' he asks.

'I really don't know!' I say and he begins to laugh too, and we laugh until tears come down my cheeks again, only this time they feel like good tears. That's when I notice the blue notebook in his hand.

'That belonged to Sid,' I say, pointing at the notebook.

'Ja,' he says and hands it to me.

I open it and look at the writing, neat and beautiful.

'Ah thought maybe you might like it. Ma father gave it to me, but somehow Ah can't bring maself to read it.'

'No, Denzel,' I say and hand it back to him. 'It was not written for me.'

'Say no more, Holly. Ah know the drill. Sorry, it was a stupid idea. Ah just want to make things better for you.'

'I know, but I do not think anyone can make it better. And maybe they are not meant to. Maybe I have to feel this bad so that I can feel good again.'

He nods and squeezes my shoulder. It is the first time I have seen a resemblance between him and Sid. It has something to do with how he touches me. But I don't say anything. Instead, I just note the similarity and allow it to sting me, as such memories do right now.

When we eventually go back inside, everyone is quieter than they were when we left and I feel a little bit uneasy. So I thank Alice for the lovely meal, say my goodbyes and leave.

I have just turned the corner outside their house when my phone rings. I look at the name on the phone and smile, immediately feeling better.

'Ah'll see you tomorrow. For sure, ja?'

'Yes, Denzel. You will see me tomorrow. For sure!' I reply.

4

Finding Inspiration

My ringing phone wakens me and I find Denzel at the other end of the line.

'Ah'm in a coffee shop that Ah reckon is about ten minutes from your place.'

'Okay. I am still in bed.'

'And you sound it. You want a coffee?'

'Yes please. Text me the place and I'll be there soon.'

'For sure.'

I hang up and pull myself out of bed. I get dressed in my clothes from yesterday and leave without looking in the mirror. I will take my chances. I find the coffee shop easily, thanks to Google Maps. I have no idea what any one did before Google Maps! When I get there I spot Denzel immediately. He laughs when he sees me.

'You look like you've just crawled out of bed.'

'I have,' I reply. 'You are up early.'

'The early bird catches the worm.'

'And am I the worm?' I say and pull a face that makes him smile. 'I am a late riser. But I go to bed late.'

'Ja, Ah was before, but not here in London. Ah guess Ah have more things to do here in the mornings. But also Ah wanted to check up on you.'

'*Pourquoi*?'

'You are not yourself.'

'Who am I, then?'

'You know what Ah mean.'

'I told you, I am going through some bad times. But if you want to check up on me and find me in a better state it is best you look later in the day.'

'Okay, Ah will remember that. You want some food?'

I shake my head. 'I would like to smoke,' I say. I had bought some cigarettes after my slip last night, having decided that today will be a smoking day, one of the few I allow myself at times such as these.

'For sure. We can go outside.' Denzel grabs hold of our coffees and leads the way.

Outside I light up, and I notice he draws in the smell.

'You miss cigarettes I see,' I say.

'Ja, but not as much as Ah like not having to smoke every five minutes. It's a great feeling not to have to be on the end of a stub for most of the day. Ja, Ah don't miss that.'

'I miss Sid,' I say.

He nods. 'Me too.'

'And it is not getting any better. Worse actually, and I am turning nasty.'

'Na, that is the wrong word. You mean something else.'

'No, I mean nasty – *méchante*.'

'Ah don't for one minute believe it. You're not nasty, Holly. Marco is nasty. Not you.'

'Mon Dieu, it is a long time since anyone mentioned that name!'

'Still no contact between you and Pia?'

I shake my head. 'She is lost to me. But I could do with her now – I mean the friend she was before the cocaine. She is the only female friend I have ever had.'

'Ja?'

I nod. 'I don't get on with women so well. I am better with men. Women do not like me.'

'Alice liked you.'

'No she didn't, Denzel!'

'What makes you say that?'

'Because she didn't. She does not like that I am single and friends with her husband. It is a female insecurity thing. It comes from the thousands of years that women had to fight for men and fight to keep them.'

'Those times must have been before my time, and passed me by, because Ah don't remember any woman ever fighting to keep me!'

'Open your eyes, Denzel. It has been happening since the cave days.'

He laughs. 'Ah don't know, Holly.'

His laughter makes me smile. 'Well I do!' The sound of his laughter takes me back to a happier time – to Ibiza, when I was a different girl to the one I am now.

'So talk to me,' he says, and so I do.

Everything spills out. Paris. How dark my painting is these days. Raphael, and how much easier life would be if I could just pretend with him, but I cannot. Denzel sits and listens as I talk on and on. After a long time I stop, having run out of words and vocabulary. When I'm finished he asks me if I feel better, and I say that I do.

'Would you like to come see the apartment?' I ask and, as if in response to my question, his phone rings.

It is his Alice: his expression tells me even before the word 'sweetheart' leaves his lips. I am jealous. Very jealous. There is a part of me that wants Denzel all to myself. I am ashamed to admit it but it is true. I hate that this other woman has his attention. This whole other life has his attention and I am beginning to realise that he cannot be for me what I need. It makes me angry and resentful, and brings into play the nasty me that Denzel said didn't exist. If only he could see the nasty Holly and not be blinded by his good opinion of me. How easily she would destroy his happiness if it meant she could have him all to herself. Yes, this bitter Holly is nasty – the right choice of word.

I listen and watch as he talks to his wife, lost in his little bubble of happiness, a tame, settled person, and I get a flashback to the Denzel in Ibiza, that wild character. I wish we were back there now, him as he was then and me with Sid. I would gladly sacrifice his life now to be able to go back to Sid. It is horrible but it is the truth. What is the use of lying to myself.

The call ends and Denzel tells me he must go, but he will see me again soon and visit the apartment. I feel disappointed and then the truth becomes obvious to me – if he had come back with me to the apartment I would have tried to seduce him. It makes me think that Alice's female intuition has tuned in to my intentions. Denzel leaves me sitting in the café and I watch as he goes. I take him in, feeling like a predator and wondering if it is grief that makes me so.

The night before, I had left Denzel's home feeling miserable and alone. I had been surrounded by love and made to sit at the end of the table. Isolated. Jutting out. Making their even number odd. That is my fate now – an odd number that would like to be even again. I wonder about my decision to come to London without Raphael, and for a time I am tempted to call him, to take back my words and ask him to join me. But I will not. It would not be fair to him. Now that I know how it feels to be in love I want to be fair to him.

I set off on foot and walk beside the river. I remember a time when Papa brought me here as a child and I had walked alongside him. I imagine Sid there in that same place with his mother. We see each other, the little him and the little me, and make a plan to meet in our futures. The little boy watches me with curiosity. His mother, the actress, is flamboyant and catches my father's roaming eye. I see it so clearly that I almost believe it to be true. This passing encounter, a promise of what was to come in Ibiza.

Papa, he says he loves women. However, he is mistaken, for he refuses to seek out just one. He desires many. Women are things to him, and things cannot be loved because affection travels in the wrong direction. It is all about the 'I' and its need for the thing. He does not give any consideration to things when he decides he must have them. But when one is truly in love, we should want the other person to be happy, regardless of our needs. I know this because I felt it for a little time. Papa feels it with me only because he has no need for me – not the way he needs other women.

Papa has many women who I do not admire. His most recent girlfriend is my age, and I wonder how he can do this and not be ashamed when they are with me. I have to remind myself that he is not subject to the same laws of decorum as ordinary people. He is, after all, an artist, as he frequently reminds me. He claims that I am an artist too, yet he seems to crave the conventional life for me. He thinks a life with Raphael would be fitting for me. Raphael is handsome, rich and loves me very much, Papa says. But I do not love him. I love Sid, and Sid is gone.

Life is this mess now.

So what of Holly Du Plessis, the artist? What is she? A philanderer like her father, perhaps? I have had many lovers. I am aware of my beauty and play it to my advantage. Most men love it and most women do not. It makes them feel threatened, just as it did Alice last night, which is a shame as we might have been friends. Denzel finds me attractive; I can tell and she can tell. But she cannot handle it and has decided that I am the enemy, as most of the women I meet do. Except Pia, but then Pia was different anyhow. We had been lovers, so I suppose she saw the real me and the illusion collapsed. I am human and, despite what I look like on the outside, the inside is just the same bloody mess as everybody else.

I think back to Alice and remember her reaction to me. Why are women like that? Perhaps I would be the same in her place if I felt I were competing with another woman for Sid's attention. I like to think not, but I am probably no different to all the women who annoy me so easily. I am tempted to torture Alice for her silliness. Because of her, my friendship with Denzel will not be as free-flowing as I would like it to be. *Non.* She will make sure to put obstacles in the way. But perhaps she is right to feel threatened: the truth is, I am drawn to Denzel, especially now that I know he is Sid's brother. And it would be easy to confuse this feeling for something else. Denzel could be a tangible substitute for Sid, allowing me to satisfy my longing for Sid and fill up the void. But this is nonsense, for inside I know the truth: it would not fill the void, only deepen it.

Tim Harris had charmed me, telling me that he could he see why his son loved me. I wonder what was at the root of his statement. Did he see something more in me? The real person? The artist? Or did he see what most men see – a physical body that is desirable by the standards of a man-made culture. I had been declared beautiful as a child, and the woman I became was equally pleasing. It is a blessing in this modern world where the physical beauty I possess is admired and revered (and I know how to use it!). But it is also a curse. Like now, for example. I have stopped walking and I can see a man watching me, making plans to approach; so I move forward before he finds the courage. He does not follow, thankfully. Right now I do not want to play the game of seduction.

Today is a day for my imagination, I remind myself as I will my busy mind to be quiet so that I can see outside of myself and discover what it is I want to create. Where will it begin? What will be the first idea to spark all the rest? What will soon appear on my canvas is out there waiting to be captured. This knowledge excites me, so much so that I feel myself rise above my sadness and my troubles. I wonder what others do to move on from such feelings, for not everyone chooses artistic creation as a way to escape. However, the feeling is short-lived as my mind travels back to Sid. I picture him walking here as a man, beside me, showing me his homeland.

Sid and I never spoke about past loves – there was no time – but he had said he never felt a love like ours before. I believed him and told him that our connection was a first for me too. Perhaps he would have walked here dreaming of me, as I walked in Paris dreaming of him. Deep down I did dream of meeting a boy who would knock me off my feet. I think maybe every girl does that a little bit as she grows up, even if some do not admit it. But I cannot be sure. I am just one in a trillion billion million girls.

I pass the Tate and decide to go inside and watch through the world of modern art. It does not interest me in relation of my own work, but it is good to look at what others are doing. Papa has always preached this and I believe him, just as I do with most things, especially about art. I am just about to go inside when my phone rings. It is Papa, as if my thoughts have summoned him. I wonder if Bebe has been in contact with him and told him of my wandering.

'*Bonjour*, Papa,' I say.

'Holly, what are you doing?' Today Papa is in English. It seems that my French connections are adapting to my new environment.

'I decided to come to London for a while. It is not okay?'

'I don't know. Are you okay? Bebe is worried.'

'I am not okay, but I am here to get okay. I need to find some inspiration, that is all.'

'You are in the Tower Bridge apartment?'

'Of course! Where else would I go!'

'Do you want me to come?'

'*Non*, Papa. I am fine, really.'

'You are sure?'

'Yes. This will make me feel better. How is New York?'

'It is good. A lot of interesting people. But soon I will come back to Paris. And I might stop off at London before.'

'Great! But not now. London is just for me now.'

'But you are alone!'

'And that is how I want to be. Okay?'

'Okay. But, Holly, you will call me if you need anything. Yes?'

'Of course, Papa!''

'*Je t'aime, ma chérie.*'

'*Je t'aime*, Papa.'

We end the call and I begin to cry, my loneliness getting the better of me. I cry into my hands, and that is when the inspiration comes to me. Hands and feet in all their forms. I look at the foot of the building in front of me and I imagine the feet digging into the ground; and the building's hands are there overhead, pulling it up towards the sky. I have the beginning of an idea, and now the magic will present itself. What I need to fall on to my canvas will come my way as it always does. The spell is cast!

I enter the Tate with a new-found excitement, knowing I had done the right thing in leaving Paris. I feel creation coming to life, vital and ready, as I walk through the rooms of the gallery taking everything in. There is an exhibition by a Brazilian sculptor I have not heard of and I eat up his work. Although it is more abstract than I like, my head fills in the details of his linear structures. They become limbs all grabbing towards me, but in the most seductive of ways, wanting to touch me, shape me into understanding what they mean and why they exist. The metal structures are black, in stark contrast to the bright white of the walls, but my mind creates a myriad of colours, all psychedelic and clashing. Wonderful! I'm alive and now I want to leave, to no longer be in someone else's creative world but return to my own. I go outside.

The sun feels warm on my skin and I breathe in the fresh air. My urge to paint heightens. I set off in the direction of home at an almost frenzied pace, impatient to get back, my hands itching to begin. It is almost like I'm possessed, and it is growing inside me and leading me to the blank canvas waiting for me to bring it to life. I run the final length of road, feeling like a little child, almost knocking over a young man but not stopping, only calling back my apology and feeling his eyes on me as I run. I am drawn to where I now belong. I must begin now. The images are passing through my head in quick succession, one after the other. I must capture them while they are fresh. Run, Holly.

I get home and cast off my clothes as I hurry up the hallway so that I am naked by the time I get to the studio. There, I find one of my oversized t-shirts with the soft cotton and slip it on. This is how I like to paint – almost naked, with a thin layer of clothing sitting erotically on my naked flesh. I feel the charge, and my nipples harden under the fabric as my memory reawakens and takes me back to Ibiza.

I had never sketched Sid's hands or feet, but as I close my eyes I find the images in my memory bank, all stored waiting for me to bring them to life. I feel his hands first, and then I remember them as they traced the contours of my body. He had lain with me that first morning and traced the curves of my body from head to toe; it had tickled. But I held back my laughter, allowing it to further intensify the sensual feeling.

Now I can feel his hands again as if they are outlining my body and I remember the curves of those hands – the beautiful wrists, the curl of the fingers, long with well-defined bones. I pick up a pencil and begin to sketch quickly, not thinking too much, just feeling. I sketch his hands in all positions, angle after angle, pages and pages of them. I sketch through the night until the sun begins to rise from over the bridge. I watch in awe as the pages grow, feeling like I am everything, yet also only a little speck in this beautiful planet. Then pure exhaustion takes hold of me and gently lays me down and whispers for me to sleep. And so I do.

5

Brushstrokes And Björk

My father, the great artist Jean-Claude Du Plessis, was once asked by a French journalist how he paints, and he replied 'one brush stroke at a time'. I fell in love with that idea. It is simple and it is true, for that is how any picture is created.

My love of painting is, without question, genetic, handed down from my papa; it is in my blood. But I have also been surrounded by paints and brushes since I was very young. So I grew to love them early on. Papa had me painting as a tot. He himself started in his teens without anyone to show him. He spent a whole afternoon surrounded by Monet's paintings and decided he would be an artist too. And that is what he did.

Working a day job to fund his new-found passion, my papa taught himself to paint, and within a decade he was one of Paris's most acclaimed artists. It is amazing, really! And now his passion lives on in me. I am following in his footsteps, and my papa says it makes him very proud. Of course, my early life has been charmed, unlike his. I have made the most of it and, at times, taken it for granted. Sometimes it is easy to forget our many blessings until something reminds us. Bebe became a mother to me while my father lived a solitary life, keeping his many girlfriends away from his family. He says that is how he likes it. When I try to suggest that he is missing out – on family life, on stable, committed relationships – he assures me that, however things look from the outside, he is content with his life as it is, for he is a person meant to be alone. For the longest time I believed that I was the same. I had not experienced any deep connections, only boys treating me as a thing to be possessed – the same behaviour as I had seen my whole life in Jean-Claude – and I would use them for sex only, satisfying my needs and amusing me with their shallow and predictable natures.

But then I met Sid and something was different. Here was a boy who wanted to know me, who was interested in all of me and believed me to be the person he had been waiting for. It had taken me by surprise and completely knocked the breath out of me. Although we made love only a handful of times, we had discovered the depth of each other. I had never been with someone like that before. It was not like it is with Raphael, the skilful lover who took my virginity when it was offered. However, when I was with Sid it was as if all my other experiences disappeared. This was new, almost like two virgins clumsy in their mutual desire to please the other, to love the other, above all else. And now, as I remember us making love, I picture our hands and feet as we connected. I feel an ache in my heart as I realise that I may never have this again with anyone, that perhaps Sid was the first and the last. Why had this happened to me? And would I give it all back not to feel this loss now? I let all my emotions flow on to the canvas, a safe place for this energy, and feel strong in my ability to channel it into my work. It will sustain me as I find my feet in London.

I am painting in the dead of night now. My earlier drawings have unearthed the painting that is developing in front of me. Brushstroke after brushstroke, just as Jean-Claude said. I place the intense energy where it belongs, connecting me to my lost love as if the canvas is fusing us together again. I remember Sid that first time in the café when we sat chatting nervously. His hands were shaking as he spoke, giving him away. How much they can reveal!

Eventually he had told me he liked me in the sweetest way, almost like a little boy in a schoolyard, and then later he had asked if he could kiss me, and he did. His kiss had lingered on my lips for days after – I promise, it is true! As we sat facing each other, we had piled our hands like a tower between us on the table and sat there forehead to forehead. Our hands together, connecting us. The heat of our palms almost melting us into each other. I remember now and close my eyes, resurrecting the feeling.

'Are you with me, Sid?' I ask into the thin air. 'Are you here?'

Silence.

Denzel confessed that he had conversations with Sid and often felt that his brother was there in the room with him. But I have had no such comfort. My conversations have all felt one-sided, confirming for me that there is no afterlife. We die and that is it: The End. Sid is gone from me forever, his energy back in the ether. It is part of what I connect to when I paint; it overwhelms my body, letting me wear it like a cosy sweater as I try to express it with paint and brush. Now I imagine us making love here in London, in this apartment; me discovering his hands and feet, together again as if life had never intervened and pulled us apart. The memory of him is alive inside my body. As I paint, it pulls me apart at the centre, unwrapping me and opening me up.

'Make me pregnant with you,' I say out loud. 'I want all of you inside me.'

That tremendous feeling: him as close to me as he could get but me wanting him closer. The feeling that I could remove my skin so we could be one. To swallow him whole and have him inside me. As I paint I think of life beating hard and fast through me. I continue brushstroke after brushstroke until the picture is done, and then I leave the studio.

Fully awake now, despite the darkness, I turn to music, to one of my favourite albums. In the cold dark night there is just me and *Vespertine*. I first heard this album when my best friend Ari died. This was when my admiration for Björk turned into complete awe. Here was an artist that could make me see music much like painting. Her beats seemed to be able to go anywhere, just like my blank canvas, and she could make the music swirl around me like manic brushstrokes dancing through the air.

I listen until, unable to stay still any more, I am on my feet twirling around the big room that overlooks Tower Bridge. I dance and remember that I love to dance. I have not danced for the longest time. Why have I not done my favourite thing for such a long time? It's something I can do with ease at anytime. I move as if I am remembering my body and what it is capable of. I twist and turn and move my limbs this way and that, movements that take me all the way back to the ballet lessons of my early years, when I discovered the joy of movement. It had been suggested then that I could be a dancer, but even then I knew what I was, who I was. I was always only ever going to be a painter. Just like Jean-Claude.

I had taken what I needed from those lessons, and dancing has been a big part of my life ever since. But Ari was the dancer. My first best friend, Ari, had died in a car crash when we were teenagers. It was the biggest shock of my life – before I lost Sid. Ari was there one minute and gone the next. We did everything together as children. His father was another artist, one of Papa's few friends, so Ari and I had been forced upon each other from an early age. But neither of us minded as we were similar and had much in common, given our bohemian fathers. We loved each other, and we were about as close as two friends can get. My beautiful Ari, the dancer and companion of my early years. I spin with him now, feeling as if the music is charged with his memory.

Ari used to float through the air as if he was suspended by an invisible thread. How I loved him! He was like no one else. I was entranced by his beautiful body and how he moved it. Before I loved him for how he was, I loved him for how he looked, I remember now, and it dawns on me as I dance: I am as guilty as everyone else. Deep down I am no different – shallow, focused on the surface. What else can you expect when you are raised by a father who constantly told you you were the prettiest little girl he had ever seen and who puffed out his chest like a peacock when others noticed me. Always we are swayed by what the eyes see. And, of course, is that not the purpose of most art? To give expression to the great beauty we see in front of us? Perhaps everything comes back to beauty. It is what many people in this world worship above everything else.

As I dance I am with Ari again, remembering the times when we would dance together. He loved to dance with me for he could lift me easily and I would go where he needed me to go almost instinctively. We spent many days and nights dancing until he was taken away from me. On the awful night when the news came, I went to Raphael who quelled the devastation in me by feeding desires I didn't know I had. He took me to ecstasy, my first time, and it had been spectacular and made me believe that I was born to have sex. I had read many stories about it being painful and a let-down for many girls. But it wasn't for me; I had an experienced lover who took my body to orgasm easily. As I dance, I feel the charge of the memory and long for Raphael to do his magic now. The knowledge that he is miles away makes my longing for him grow, and then my mind goes to someone closer to hand – to Denzel. My eyes fly open in alarm as if the thought itself is a betrayal. Sid's brother! How inappropriate that would be, especially now that he has created a new life with Alice. But it is also a satisfying thought. I wonder if he thinks about it too.

The fantasy is set loose and I remember how wild Denzel was in Ibiza, like a fire in danger of burning everything around it. His addiction fuelled his destruction and pushed him close to the edge of his existence, just like Pia. And then in Paris, I had felt the same charge. But when he told me he was Sid's brother, that changed everything between us – everything. It would have felt disrespectful to the memory of my love if we had done anything together. It is crazy, really! Who would have thought I would develop these morals, if that is what they are. But now they are wavering under the great strain of my longing and this bitterness.

I dance on as I remember Sid, my Sid, the boy who stole my heart and made love to me like no one had ever done before. He gave me the whole of his heart and demanded that I give him no less. And I had. In Ibiza, Pia had introduced me to the club scene. It was perfect except for one thing: groping hands often made dancing impossible and made me angry. Why was it that men felt they could take hold of me while I expressed my need to move? I have never understood it and hated it all my life, cursing those girls who allow men to believe it is okay, and that creative expression is an open invitation for sex. My voice grew tired from shouting in those days. But I could always dance like this alone, as I do now.

Björk sings on and on and I dance, matching the intensity of her every beat. And when she finishes I am satisfied and exhausted, with only one thought in my head: how good it is to be alive at such moments as these.

6
Familiar Hands

I first notice him because I feel the weight of his stare as he watches me have my afternoon coffee at the café where I had met Denzel a few days earlier.

He is sitting with his hands wrapped around his coffee cup. Somehow the process of creation has drawn me to these hands, so like the hands I have been sketching for the past three days. My work has been furious; I have been rediscovering my time with Sid in hand movements. But now I need a model, real living hands to bring the work to life. And I seem to have found them, or have they found me?

The stranger has facial hair, which has the promise of becoming a full-blown beard but for now is just a shadow. I watch him; he does not take his eyes off me. I am the first to look away. When I look back he is still watching me. I wonder if his eyes are navy blue like Sid's, although something tells me they are brown, almost black. And then I remember that Sid's eyes looked black at times. And then I think of Tim Harris's half-smile, the same smile he had passed on to his son. These are the memories of a face that you know intimately because you have looked at it so intensely as you painted every feature, a face with which you had fallen in love.

As I watch this stranger now I wonder if there is a possibility of love again. I feel the ache in my heart and desperately clutch for the answer I want to hear more than anything in this world: yes, it can happen again, and there might be a chance that it is sitting at the table across from me. This longing for someone draws me towards him, pulling me as if I am on the end of a leash. I have no resistance.

I walk over to his table, bringing my coffee with me, aware that he is watching my every move. He looks at me and cocks his head ever so slightly.

'Excuse me,' I say and wait a moment to see if he will respond. He doesn't. 'Can I join you?' I continue.

He nods and I sit down. Still he says nothing and I am hooked. He is breathtaking close up and I immediately want to draw him. It is like how I had felt in Ibiza. Something of this man is Sid even though his colouring is different and he is taller and broader. But the hands. The eyes. The feeling. It is Sid.

'My name is Holly,' I say and extend my hand, wanting to touch him. He does not move but I hold my hand in front of him just in case.

'Adam,' he says, still not moving.

I drop my hand.

His voice surprises me. I had expected him to sound like Sid, I suppose. I sit there, not knowing what to say now. I want to ask if I can paint him but I feel intimidated in a way I am not used to. Usually men react positively to me, but he does not. He does not seem to notice me that way. Perhaps he is gay. But even gay men react to me in a good way, delighted rather than seduced. But not this one. This Adam, he is indifferent and it stings me for I want him to notice me, to feel attracted to me, just as I am attracted to him. I look down, no longer wanting to subject myself to his stony stare, and catch sight of the guitar case on the floor beside him.

'You are a musician!' I say before I can stop myself.

He nods.

He is hard work and offers nothing so I must take what I can. 'You sing?' I ask.

He nods again.

'Where?'

'In the shower.' His accent is not English.

'I do not understand!' I reply.

He looks at me as if I am stupid and I can feel my cheeks redden.

'I busk outside,' he says eventually.

I wonder what that has to do with the shower but decide not to ask, for something tells me that he will be mean. 'So I can hear you soon?' I ask instead.

'Not today. I'm done for today.'

'When?'

He shrugs.

'Your accent is not English,' I say.

'Neither is yours.'

'French,' I offer.

He nods once.

'And yours?' I ask

'Irish.'

'Do you live in London?'

'For now.'

It hits me suddenly, a feeling like I know him or we have been here before. 'Do I know you from somewhere?' I ask.

He shakes his head. 'I'm not from anywhere you'd ever have been, Holly from France. You don't belong where I've come from.'

'Is that good or bad?' I ask and smile my most charming smile.

'It's neither good nor bad. Just a fact,' he says flatly.

'I have a question for you,' I say and he looks at me, waiting. He is so intense, I am almost drunk on the tension. It is most arousing. But nothing in his behaviour suggests he is feeling the same way. I wonder how he would react if I were to ask him to have sex with me. 'Can I paint you?' I ask.

'What colour?'

I begin to laugh. 'Blue,' I tell him. Blue was Sid's favourite colour.

'Like a big Smurf,' he says.

It makes me laugh, but he still doesn't even smile.

'I would like you to be my subject,' I say eventually.

'Your subject!' He is teasing me now – I can hear it in his voice – and my face reddens again. He sees this but does nothing to ease my embarrassment. He is cold, impenetrable. But something of him is escaping and hooking me in.

'Yes,' I say eventually. 'My model, if you prefer.'

'Jaysus, that's just as bad! How much?'

'I am not sure,' I say. 'I never know how long it will take.'

'No, not how long. How much money do you pay?'

My embarrassment grows. 'I have never paid anyone before,' I say. There is something wrong here.

'That's not very professional,' he says.

This makes me angry. Usually I would react, but I do not with him because I want to win him over, to break down his barriers and make him want me.

'How much do you want?' I ask, ignoring everything other than my desire for him.

He shrugs. 'I earn about twenty pounds an hour from busking. So let's say the same, since you'll be denying me potential earnings of that amount.'

'Okay, it is settled,' I say. 'Can you start tomorrow at about two o'clock?'

'Sure.'

'I live not far from here. So we can meet here?'

He nods.

I drink the last of my coffee in silence. For the first time I think I might understand Papa's women a little better. He makes them feel this way. I have seen it, and I have sworn that I will never let a man treat me that way. Yet here I am, and in spite of myself I want to go further. I am hooked. I want him. But this is different to how I wanted Sid because Sid wanted me back. This man has no desire for me whatsoever; in fact I think he dislikes me, even though I have done nothing to deserve that. Maybe he is a misogynist. I have met many of them, but even they have shown more of an interest than he has. His dislike feels personal, as if I have done something to him, even though we did not know each other before now.

I wait for him to say something to keep me here, but he doesn't. He sits in silence, letting me know that we are done and I should leave. So I do.

I say goodbye and he waves me off with an exaggerated hand movement, mocking me. As I stand up, I feel extremely self-conscious, which is something I am not used to. I worry that I will stumble as I leave but thankfully I do not. I make it out of the café without losing my footing, but there is something different about how I walk, as if I am skulking away from him. I feel his eyes on me, but not in the way I usually feel men watch me, as if they are under my spell. Today, I am the one captivated.

I think about him as I walk the distance back to the apartment. He had reminded me of Sid, most definitely. That was what had drawn me to him. However, his arrogance was similar to my papa's. I would never have thought it would be attractive to me, yet I want this Adam, and it feels wonderful to want someone again, to really want them. I begin to feel excited, truly excited, as if the future might not be as bleak as I had thought. As I walk home there is something new inside me. There is hope.

7

Adam's Eyes: Part I

These days, I walk on foreign ground. It's the first time I have been out of my homeland. I am here to meet my maker. It all feels very biblical and I wonder if that's because I've been raised by a family of God-fearing people. I've no idea what'll happen. I just know that I needed to come here, to bring all the pieces of my life together like a jigsaw puzzle, in the hope that I can make some sense of it. Understanding is so important to me. I'm eighteen according to my passport. A friend of a friend helped me with that and all I had to do in return was deal some drugs. It's big business in Dublin these days. I sold them in school. It was easy, really. I supplied to fools older than me, knowing I would never make their mistake. Idiots! I'm fifteen going on thirty. My childhood ended a long time ago. Nothing ages you like death and the truth.

Death came first ...

The woman who raised me, the one I called Mother, died. She died when I least expected it and when I was most dependent on her. It was cruel. And ugly. Cancer. No one should have to go through that. No one should have to watch their loved ones suffer. It was hell. How she was and what was taken from her was shocking. It shook me to the core and I'll probably never be able to wipe those images from my head. Ever.

And then the truth ...

Afterwards, I discovered where I really came from. I discovered that the woman I called Mother was not my birth mother but my grandmother. The woman who actually gave birth to me was someone I'd been calling my sister all my life. Poison Marie, filled with the venom my father deposited inside her, conceived me after she was raped. He took what he wanted from her and gave her me in return. I've only known about this for a short time, but somehow I've always known it deep down. It's been written on every twisted look Marie's ever thrown my way as I grew up.

My 'blood' father is Denzel Anderson. That I found him so easily is still amazing to me. But that's the price of celebrity: you can be located without too much difficulty in this vast world if you're at all famous. I learned this piece of important information from the telly. What are the chances! My father and my grandfather were at the BAFTAs, which we were watching one night on TV. Poison Marie saw them and had another breakdown there and then (she had her first breakdown shortly after her saint of a husband, John, died in a hit and run). My aunt Bernie, who I'd thought was my sister up to that point, tried to shut her up but couldn't. Marie announced that she'd been raped by the man on the telly and she was tired of staying quiet because it was an awful injustice, what had happened, and being made to watch the little bastard grow up right in front of her. It didn't take a whole lot of brainpower to work out who 'the little bastard' was, especially as the person she was pointing at on the screen looked suspiciously like me. Even I could see it!

So I am the spawn of famous people. If I was fazed by such things that might be a big deal, but I'm not. It's meaningless to me. I'm more interested in people who do incredible things in this world rather than the wastes of space who make 'art' about it, claiming it changes everything. It changes nothing. Only action changes things. Direct action. Save a life, don't write about saving one. It's really that simple for me. I've always believed that, and that one day I'll do something that'll make a difference. I'd pick a noble profession and be like Paddy Sheehan, the man I thought was my father. I'd never met him, but I felt I knew him thanks to my mother – my grandmother – who kept his memory alive all through my childhood. He was a guard – an Irish policeman – and had dedicated his whole life to protecting the people who lived in his city. The plan was that I would do the same and make him proud, if he were alive. And Mammy too.

But then this awful discovery: my real father on the screen and Marie behaving in a way I had never seen before. In fairness I can understand why. Denzel Anderson had raped her and fucked her up, and yet there he was, on the screen making big news as if nothing had happened. His life had simply continued, and it appeared to be a good life – a prosperous life. But it wasn't so for Marie Sheehan. His actions took her spirit and broke her. What an ordeal she had to endure, especially when her mother, my grandmother, made her have me, and then raised me in the same house. Jesus, Mammy, what were you thinking? I loved you and thought you were wise, but that was one fucked up decision, don't you think! What a thing to put your daughter through! To make her look at me every day and remember the face of her rapist. No wonder she hated me. It's like a sick fairytale that demands a happy ending, whatever cost.

The next day I read online about Tim Harris's secret son. Denzel, my father, the child from Tim Harris's past that he had kept hidden away. The irony was not lost on me. And then I went in search of my new family. I found an interview that mentioned a whereabouts, Borough Market, and gave a picture of an impressive building, which I printed out. My home! I knew then that I'd head to London. I'd seek him out. There would be retribution for what he'd done.

So here I am. Finally. It wasn't easy, but I made it. And I found Denzel, my real father, and the full-of-herself French girl who has left the coffee shop just now, the girl who has asked me to be her 'subject'. Pretentious bitch! Another artist. Just what the world needs!

It's crazy, really. I'd followed her after she'd left Denzel's place and I've been watching her ever since, biding my time and planning to approach her. A few days ago she just about knocked me over as she ran along the street. She hadn't noticed me then, yet today she's approached me – handed herself to me on a silver platter.

She fancies me. I got that very quickly. Yeah, she likes me and tried to flirt with me. But that sort of thing has never much interested me, at least not in the way it seemed to interest my mates. It still doesn't. I'd wondered if that was because of my strange upbringing – a mother who'd held on to me like a replacement husband and set such high standards for me. But now I wonder if it's something to do with how I was made – some kind of poetic justice that I'm paying for the sins of my father.

I walk to my new accommodation, which is in a backstreet in the heart of the city. It's all I can afford. I've saved a lot of money but it doesn't go far in London. Busking is good here – lucrative – but still I need to watch the pennies. And I'm getting better on my guitar now that I'm playing so much. My hobby is proving to be a cash cow and means that I don't have to seek out gainful employment, which would only raise awkward questions.

I saw Denzel for the first time shortly after I found the flat that was in the picture I'd printed out. I recognised him and saw the likeness between us, at least on a physical level. I hope I'm nothing like him. I stood right beside him and he had no idea. He didn't even notice me; he was too caught up in his own world. I sat and watched him as he bought a cup of coffee and carried it back to the table only a few feet away from me. He didn't look guilty. He looked quite pleased with himself, as those with a charmed life tend to look, as if they are somehow responsible for their good turn of fortune. I wondered if he remembered what he'd done and how he justified it to himself.

As I sat and watched him, I decided the time had come to face him and I was just about to approach when she came in and knocked the wind out of me. Denzel called her Alice, but she could have been Marie Sheehan. She was the spit of her. And that wasn't the biggest shock. This woman was pregnant, and judging by the way he placed his hand on her belly and the way they were together I'd say that this is Denzel's baby Alice is carrying. He was tender with her, a tenderness my mother never knew from him. All the time they sat together, oblivious to everyone around them, I got so much information from them. It's incredible what people reveal when they're blind to the dangers that surround them. If they knew I existed they wouldn't take their eye off the ball for a second. But they'll remain oblivious to my existence, drunk on their own happiness. They seem to think that their happiness forms a protective shield around them. It doesn't. I am a danger to them both.

They left together, Denzel and Alice, and Denzel walked her home, back to the building in the magazine cutting. And then Denzel left again and I followed him to his place of work, a club called Rain Dogs. How rosy his life is, but how close it is to crumbling down! If only he knew. Then that big ugly smile would quickly drop from his big ugly face.

I waited for him to leave work. I watched and waited for a long time. Who'd have thought I could be so patient! I followed him home where I saw my grandfather kiss another man outside their front door. My grandfather is a queer! The freak show continues! I was just about to go home when the French girl showed up and a plan began to take root in my mind.

This girl could be my way in, if I play my cards right. Now the door is wide open and I am ready to walk all the way inside.

8

Blank Canvas

I get to the coffee shop early and find Adam outside playing guitar. I hear him before I see him. He plays a Spanish tune that I recognise, although I do not know its name. It is a tune I had heard on a Paco de Lucía album that Pia used to play in the apartment when we were at art school. She was a huge fan and had even taken me to see him when he played in Paris. It is a beautiful piece of music and Adam plays it very well. I stop to watch him as he plays, totally engrossed in what he is doing and detached from his surroundings, his eyes hidden behind dark glasses. He looks odd and it makes me like him even more.

Although I cannot see his eyes I recall them from yesterday – navy blue, like Sid's. I sit down, observing him keenly with my artist's eyes, and begin the process that will end with his appearance on a canvas. I wonder if he senses me as he plays. If he does, he gives no sign of it. My attention settles on his hands – what had first attracted me – and an idea strikes me. I will ask him to play today, and I will sketch his hand movements on the guitar. They look beautiful and remind me of a flamenco dancer, but perhaps that is because of the music he is playing.

My craving for coffee drives me indoors and I order, but a great deal of my attention remains focused on this Adam and his music. His facial hair and dark glasses give the appearance of someone in disguise, as if he is hiding from something – or maybe from everything – and I have an urge to see what is behind this mask that he wears. I wonder what his story is. He looks young; he's definitely younger than me, but that has never bothered me. For me, age is simply a number and more often than not a poor measure. It is not the years themselves that mature us but what we do with them. Papa has always said this and he is right. I watch Adam's face and notice that his beard has grown since yesterday. It looks fuller on his face. But is it possible that someone's hair can grow so much in a day? Maybe it is just my imagination playing tricks.

Adam joins me at 2 p.m. on the dot.

'You are punctual. That is very good,' I say.

He shrugs and sits down.

'Would you like a drink?' I ask.

'Do you not want to get going?'

'Well yes, but I thought you might like a break after playing.'

'No, I'm good,' he says.

We leave and I walk beside him in silence. It strikes me that I am taking a risk, for I do not know this person yet I am bringing him to my home in a country where nobody knows me. But somehow I trust him. Or maybe I am pretending to trust him because I do not want to face the truth – that I might be bringing him home precisely because he might be a danger to me. I am a different Holly now, one that takes more risks and does not care about the consequences. It is an unsettling thought so I push it away and go back to my original story. I trust this person and I want him to trust me too. And I want him to notice me. His indifference to me is both fiercely appealing and incredibly vexing.

Once we are inside I wait for him to react to the apartment, but there is nothing. If Adam is impressed by the place he does not say. Maybe he is good at concealing things. Or perhaps I have met one of those rare breed of people who are just not impressed by such things. Now wouldn't that be something!

I lead him straight away into the studio where I will begin working once he is settled.

'Would you like some water?' I ask.

'Yes, please,' he replies.

I get a bottle of water and a glass from the kitchen and when I return he is sitting in the exact spot I want him to be, looking relaxed and self-assured. There is something remarkably beautiful about him, man and boy within the same frame. I pour him a glass of water and hand it to him.

'I will get changed and leave you to settle in. I will sketch you in various poses,' I explain. 'What I would like is for you to play your guitar. Would that be okay?'

He nods.

'I will put on some music and maybe you can play along, *oui*?'

'Whatever. I'm on your payroll,' he says.

'Okay, I will choose something and we shall see how you get on.'

I select something specific. It is a soundtrack of Tim Harris's, probably composed around the time that Sid was born. It feels like the right thing. I leave him and take myself and my painting clothes into the bedroom. Usually I would change in the studio without a second thought, but today I feel self-conscious. This is new territory for me. I am far from self-assured near this Adam.

The music drifts into the bedroom as I remove all my clothes and slip into one of my special t-shirts made from a fabric I was drawn to first in art school, a mixture of cotton and fleece, like bedclothes. I feel the fabric against my bare skin and indulge myself for a few moments before I rejoin Adam. I am vulnerable, naked but for this fabric that shows most of my body. I like for my subjects to see me exposed and vulnerable in the hope that, charmed by my openness, they will let me see something of them. But today there is another reason. I want this man to see me and to want me just as Sid Harris had done. I want to feel his desire as I sketch, just as I had with Sid. I close my eyes and I'm back there in Ibiza but filled with the excitement of this new possibility, the idea that this man might be someone to love. *I need someone in my life now. Let it be you, Adam.* Even as I think the thought I begin to shake. *Calme-toi!*

When I come back into the room he is so engrossed in the music that he does not notice. As I begin sketching he does not look my way. The line of connection is one way and I am pulled in. As I sketch the angles jump out at me and land on the page. His hands are beautiful and the shapes his fingers create on the guitar are breathtaking. The sketches come easily, but although I am using charcoals the drawings appear green. It is odd! Maybe it is because it is a colour I sense from this man, a colour he likes. This I know, and not just because he has worn it two days running or because it suits him so well (the colour wears him somehow), but because it is in the energy that now passes from him to me.

Whether he likes it or not, I am really seeing him now. That is the privilege of the artist. He gives me so much of himself in spite of the fact that he would prefer not to. I can feel his animosity. Meanness comes off him in waves. But as he creates his music I see him. His body gives me what I need, despite his reluctant mind, and hints at what might be underneath. I get lost in him, piecing together what comes to me sporadically. The CD finishes and restarts and I let it continue. It plays through many times; I lose count as he accompanies the music of Sid's father. The creative energy of the man who made Sid is harmonising with this Adam, who reminds me more and more of the boy who stole my heart in Ibiza. His energy jumps out of him and on to my page and I am given access to it by a power that is greater than both of us. As I see him and feel him, my desire for him grows. It falls on to the page and becomes a part of the work itself.

I sketch for hours and only stop when I get to the last page of the notebook. When I look at the time I am surprised. We have been here for almost five hours.

'*Mon Dieu*!' I say, and he stops and looks at me for the first time. 'We have gone on for a long time!'

He follows my gaze to the clock on the wall. 'You owe me a hundred pounds,' he says.

It throws me totally. Is that all he has to say?

'Of course,' I reply and reach for my bag.

When I pay him he says, 'Are we done here?' and I almost feel like crying. He is rejecting me fantastically, telling me he does not care about me, that he does not want to get to know me. It almost feels like a punishment.

'Can you come tomorrow?' I ask and I can feel my lip quiver despite my efforts to stop it.

He nods and packs up his guitar. 'Sure. I'll come straight here at two. Okay?'

'Yes please,' I say.

He looks me up and down, his eyes lingering nowhere in particular. It is as if I am a blank canvas for him. Then he leaves without another word.

Alone in the studio, I begin to cry. Sid. I want Sid, now more than ever. As I listen to the music of Tim Harris play in the background, I want his son here with me where he belongs. The anger inside me comes to the surface. How is it that he was sent to me to be taken away again, leaving me like this – desperate to be loved and feeling like a hungry mouse scurrying around looking for crumbs? I hate this need in me. It is something I had not known before Sid walked into my life and blew the lid off all my defences, leaving me bare and open and alone.

This Adam feels nothing for me. He makes it clear. But the truth is, I want to penetrate all the way through to him, not because this is some sort of game that I want to win, but because I am feeling something that I have been desperate to feel for a long time. It might just destroy me if I were to lose it again.

I get an awful feeling of dread and leave the studio, not wanting this horrible, thick, debilitating energy to infect this precious creative space. Afraid of where my despair might lead me, I go to my bed where I cry until blessed sleep comes.

9

Obscene Green

Usually after I sketch someone I feel close to them, and when they leave I pick up on the vibe that is in the room and begin to paint. But today is different. Today, overwhelmed by my own emotions, I went to bed to cry away my sorrow. Now, as I stand in the studio, I can feel only myself. Adam is gone, every trace of him. My sketch pad is full of drawings of him, but he is absent. There is only me – Holly – my desperation, my need, my desire. As I look at the sketches I think that despite how I felt earlier, I had captured nothing of him. I am beginning to doubt myself and my ability to paint, but I push past it, eager to get lost in my work.

Although Adam had given me nothing of himself, it felt like the page had captured him as he poured his heart into his guitar playing. Now I try to remember that feeling and forget about Holly the artist who feels rejected, the girl who is left wanting in the space without him. I find my paint and immediately go to the colour green, the main colour in my head while I sketched him. I begin mixing and blending, finding many different shades of this colour that adorns the natural world. As I work I forget about my earlier insecurities; the energy works through me and I allow it to find whatever expression it needs. I am a vessel to be used, but today there is something else happening as I go through the process, some feeling that I cannot quite grasp.

I begin painting furiously and get lost in Adam so much so that I begin to wonder if I am in his hands rather than being guided by the spirit of creation. Perhaps he had cast a spell on me while he were here in this room. I feel out of control and obsessed. He is gone and has left with only a promise that he will return tomorrow. I hope that he does because I could not bear it if he didn't. *Mon Dieu*, I am like Raphael now: pitiful and unattractive, even to myself. It is no wonder Adam is unimpressed! I am a stupid, desperate, lonely girl pinning all her hopes of happiness on one person she has only just met, a person who does not want her. Yet how strong my will is, and how incapable I am of letting go! I am holding on, determined. I will love again. My mind goes to Denzel and Alice, and the image of them happy and in love makes my heart grow heavy, leaden with envy. It continues to fester inside me and now I have this need for someone else. I stop painting. I am on the verge of ringing Raphael just so I am not alone. He would be here in a few hours if I asked him to. But after he had comforted me I would want him gone and that is desperately unfair on him, a cat and mouse game. I have to pull myself through this the only way I know how. I do what has kept me sane over the past year: I paint and I lose myself in the brushstrokes. I paint until I am no longer in this world and even my wanting, which had been all-consuming, disappears. I am nothing. I do not exist. All that is left of me is an imprint of me, like a footprint left by someone who has passed by a long time ago.

I paint until I am exhausted and then I leave the room without looking at the canvases. I will do that in the morning when I will have some distance from them to really see them. I remove my t-shirt, now covered in paint, and get into the shower. I stay there for the longest time, enjoying the feeling of the hot water on my body and I stay in the moment, not daring to think about anything else. And then, when I am in danger of washing my skin away, I leave the shower and dry off.

I get dressed and go to the kitchen where I make a sandwich and eat it greedily. Then I remember that I had eaten nothing all day. *Mon Dieu!* I forget to eat too often, something else that this last bastard year has brought. I collapse on to my bed not knowing the precise time, only that it is very late – or very early, depending on your viewpoint, I suppose. I drop into a deep sleep full of Adam, then Sid and lastly Denzel. Surprisingly, it is Denzel who eventually fucks me, but it is the wild Denzel of Ibiza with his long hair.

The dream wakens me. I am hot and horny, and as I bring myself to orgasm, the Denzel of my dream remains in my head. We are both out of control in this fantasy that I had first played through when I painted him back in Ibiza. I wonder if he was aware of how tempted I was back then. I had wanted him, but his struggle had presented itself as I studied him closely. At the time, I was well acquainted with the horror of addiction. I witnessed it in Pia, so despite Denzel's muscular body and the seductive smile dancing on his huge lips that I imagined would be heaven to suck into, I had kept a safe distance. But I had wanted him, and when he left I did pretty much what I am doing now and the orgasm had been intense. As it is now. I moan into the emptiness and allow the quick surges to burst all through me. There is nothing like pleasure to shift the dark moods. I know this well having fucked away some of my worst moments with Raphael.

When I have taken as much orgasm as I can, I head into the lounge feeling completely satisfied and cleansed. I open the curtains revealing the view of Tower Bridge. The traffic tells me it is near midday and a glance at the clock confirms it. Noon on the dot and only two hours to Adam.

There is time to look and see what yesterday's work brought. I walk into the studio and it is extraordinary! I am astonished. It is as if this work belongs to another painter. I do not recognise it at all and it scares me. I wonder if there might be something wrong with me. Maybe I am growing mad like many painters. I get an overwhelming urge to speak to Jean-Claude for some assurance. There is a time difference, but my papa keeps crazy hours, sometimes painting through the night and into the early morning. I call his number and he answers.

'Holly! Is everything all right?' He sounds worried.

'Papa, I painted all day yesterday and the work is not familiar to me. It is as if someone else painted the picture. I don't see myself at all. Is this normal?'

'*Chérie*, it is truly wonderful. You are the artist, my child,' he says, and I have never felt prouder. 'Explain it all to me from the beginning.'

'I did all the usual rituals, Papa, and I did not feel like painting but I painted anyway. I left the studio like I was high or something. And then when I returned this morning I was shocked. It was like someone else had been in the room.'

'*Ma chérie*, that is wonderful. You are painting now. It all begins from here.' I could hear him yawn.

'Papa, you are on your way to bed?'

'*Oui*, I painted all night here in the Big Apple.'

'I will let you go to sleep. Sweet dreams, Papa.'

'*Je t'aime, ma chérie.*'

'*Et toi*, Papa.'

After our short call, I go back into the room to look at the work again. The pictures are amazingly vivid, all in shades of green, which look powerful and almost psychedelic in the bright light of day. There are five canvases; all are eye-catching but it is the one in the centre, as if it has claimed its rightful place, that pulls me closer.

My papa had mentioned the Big Apple and this is what I think of now as I gaze at the green sphere with two hands wrapped around it, cradling it as if it is the most sacred of objects. Jean-Claude had called me an artist; for me there is no greater accreditation, and as I look at my work, I understand it to be true.

10

On The Periphery

He arrives at 2 p.m. on the dot, just as punctual as Sid had been back in Ibiza. However, that is where the similarity ends. These are different times and a different Holly. At the door, I reach out to embrace him but he backs away, so I pull back, hurt, and probably noticeably so. He walks in and goes straight to the studio as if our roles are reversed and he is the one who lives here. The paintings from yesterday are concealed, not yet ready for others' eyes.

I bring him some water and he thanks me.

'Would you like me to play today?' he asks.

'No, not today,' I reply. 'I want us to try something different.'

He shrugs, wanting me to be in no doubt about his disregard for what we are doing.

'Do you always leave your glasses on?' I ask.

'I take them off when I sleep.'

'So that you can see your dreams?'

'I don't dream – just sleep.'

'That is a very sad thing if it is true. What music do *you* like? Yesterday I indulged myself. Today I would like you to choose something.'

'You think you might have any of the music I like here?'

'Yes, I do.' I lift up my iPod and hand it to him.

He scrolls through it, picks something and hands it back.

'Nick Drake. He is quite wonderful,' I say.

Adam acts as if he has not heard. I set my mini jukebox in its dock and get to work as the first notes of 'Time Has

Told Me' begin to play. It is perfect for my mood today. As I listen, I remember another time in my life. This is the music that had seen me through art school in Paris, a time fixed firmly in my past, and yet here it is in the present. I begin to sketch and Adam keeps his glasses on. I had hoped he might remove them, taking my hint, but no, and I get the feeling that he does it to offend me, as he seems to do many things. He watches out the window as I sketch him. Today I capture his whole form. My idea of hands and feet is no longer so pressing, especially now that something else seems to have taken control in my studio. I am totally submissive to the work, but perhaps to him personally too. I get the same uneasy feeling that I get when danger is close by, which is not surprising as I am beginning to realise that he may be as much of a threat to me as any other hazard in the outside world.

He is damaged, and I wonder what has made him like this. What woman has hardened his heart? Perhaps his mother failed him. I think about my father. His mother, my grandmother, had been a long time dead when I eventually came along, but he has told me a little about her. She had not supported his art but had been very quick to change her mind when he got famous. She got on side once the money started coming; a gold-digger. Many of the women my papa has encountered over the years seem to have followed this pattern, including my own mother. I think of her now and feel ashamed. I met her only once in my adult life when, at Papa's insistence, I went to stay with her and her new family for a while. But it had ended in disaster. She was still a gold-digger, and she only came after me to spite my father and try to tap into his fortune. *Incroyable!* I told her that I never wanted to see her again and she had honoured my request. It is the only thing for which I thank her.

Adam sits in silence. Despite remaining a reluctant subject, his body tells his story. He is hunched and restrained, as if he is carrying a load rather than sitting at rest. As I sketch he is engrossed by what is outside, lost in the view as well as his own headspace. I wonder what he is thinking, but I must let go of all personal thoughts if I am to work. Holly with her great need must disappear completely. As I let go, I drop into this strange zone that I visited yesterday, but today I am conscious of the transition as I move through. Somehow my reality changes. It feels as if I might be able to manipulate what is around me, as if I am now part of what is supernatural. It is an extraordinary feeling, almost celestial, as if I am travelling in some other realm. And that is when I feel Sid for the first time since he left. I cannot see him, yet I know he is here beside me; I no longer feel the loss of him. I look at the space where he is and the air seems to alter and become visible. He is appearing to me and yet I cannot bear it; to see him would be too much. I hate the thought that he might still exist away from me. I prefer my own version of how it is: he is gone, dead, and only the memories are left. So I close my eyes, blocking him out and breathing deeply until the feeling subsides.

The music moves on to the next Nick Drake album on my iPod, *Pink Moon*, and I finally open my eyes. There is nothing; no Sid. Adam shifts position on the sofa and draws my attention away from the emptiness. Once again I begin to draw, forgetting what has just happened. I let it disappear and concentrate solely on the lines and curves being formed on the page in front of me. Papa had said on the phone that I was the artist now and my heart swells as I remember. I am the artist and, as I forget about myself once again, a charge runs through me that feels like it could lift me off my feet.

Today the session is shorter, and once we are done I pay him and he leaves, saying that he will come again at two o'clock tomorrow. I waste no time. After a quick bite to eat I return to my canvas, eager to paint. I begin mixing colours and an extraordinary thing happens: they all have hints of green, no matter what colours I use. *Impossible*! I wonder if it is a trick of the light or my own eyes, but as I paint I become more convinced that the green is there because my canvas wants to have this colour. I wonder about the significance of that but put the notion to the back of my mind. I will question it another time. Right now the work wants to come, all the way through the canvas, and I trust that meaning will reveal itself to me when the time is right.

I paint, allowing my arm to travel in circles, and all the time I listen to the music of Nick Drake, what my subject had chosen to listen to. The shapes appear on the canvas and I paint on, allowing the pictures to be created and all the time feeling almost intoxicated by the mystery and the great promise behind it. What is happening to me? I do not know, but I am captivated by this strange feeling that I don't quite understand. I just go with it, as I must with these things, for if I think too much the charge will be broken. The work comes to life now, guiding my hand in the right direction.

Then a strange thing happens: the brush switches to my other hand. I swear it feels as if it almost jumps, even though I know my other hand is responsible, not the brush itself. I begin to paint with my right hand. It has a completely new feel and makes me travel in another direction. I follow without knowing or seeing, and with no sense of impatience to get to the end. I take my time with each brushstroke, each one leading to the next until I am exhausted and in need of food and water.

I leave the studio charged by what I have just done and tingling all over my body. It is like nothing I can ever remember feeling before without the assistance of some drug, and although it feels like something energising it also has in its make-up an element of malignancy, as if it might be capable of destroying me and swallowing me whole. It is not the feeling itself that makes me afraid, but the realisation that deep down I might just want it to come and wipe me out, completely and for good.

11
Naked Desire

It happens again the next day. I look at my work and it enchants me. It is as if it belongs to someone else and I am merely appreciating. The greens on each canvas are quite remarkable and I realise my eyes had not been deceiving me yesterday – even where I had used different colours there is a hint of green; green is everywhere. I had sketched his form yesterday, his clothed form. But today I want more. I want to sketch his naked body. The canvas demands it, as if the work itself is reaching for what it wants. It is true that I desire him as a woman, but this is about what I am creating. Yes, I am an artist, Papa, carved from the same stone as you.

As I am getting ready to have a shower the phone rings.

'*Bonjour*,' I say, forgetting myself for a minute.

'*Buenos días*, Holly!'

'Denzel, we are no longer in Ibiza. How about some French?'

'It's all the same, isn't it!'

'How are you?' I ask.

'I'm good. And you?'

'Yes. I am painting up a storm.'

'Great! Can you come out to play later?'

'How later?' I ask.

'Tomorrow night.'

'That is later! Alors, today is Friday. Tomorrow is Saturday, so it should be possible.' Given the intensity of my work over the past two days, and my suspicion that today will be no different, I decide I will take the weekend off – perhaps even Monday – to recharge. 'Where are we going?'

'We've got someone playing at the club and Ah thought you might like to come check it out.'

'That sounds great, Denzel. What time?'

'The show starts at eight-ish.'

'Then I will be there at eight-ish.'

'Great, Holly. Ah look forward to seeing you!'

'Yes, me too, Denzel.'

Once I have showered and had a coffee I wait until the doorbell rings at two on the dot. Today I don't make the mistake I made yesterday; I let Adam in and keep my distance. A few minutes later I bring water and prepare myself to ask the question.

'Today I need for you to pose differently,' I say.

'You want me naked,' he says simply.

I nod.

'Okay.'

And just like that he begins to remove his clothes. He takes everything off with such self-assurance that it almost takes my breath away. I stay and watch, hoping to see some hint of self-consciousness, but I don't. His body is beautiful, but what is even more attractive is how he carries it, as if he has spent many lifetimes with it. Naked and yet not fazed in the slightest by my presence, he possesses the beauty of youth without any sense of vulnerability or sentimentality about his youth. I think now of my father who has spent a lifetime cultivating a disregard for other people; this boy seems to have it in front of him. Sid did not have this. I suppose it is a sort of arrogance. I remember how self-conscious he had been when I painted him; I had loved that about him and it had melted me away. It had captivated me, but a different way to how this Adam is captivating me. I am hooked, as I had been in Ibiza. However, with Sid I had felt safe and just a little anxious about giving my heart away. But with Adam

I am afraid, and the fear is pronounced and huge, for I can tell that he is drawn towards his own darkness just as most are pulled towards the light. But the seed has been planted in me and I stubbornly want to bring it to full fruition, regardless of the consequences.

He stands in front of me, naked except for his glasses, and then he removes them too. Despite the fact that I have seen a lot of naked men before I feel embarrassed. There is something about how he presents himself that makes me feel lacking. And while he looks at me I maintain eye contact, although my eyes want to travel all over him, especially to what is hanging between his legs.

'You'll need to look at me if you want to sketch me,' he jeers.

'I ... I ... I don't want to make you feel uncomfortable,' I say.

'Don't worry about me. I'm not the one who's uncomfortable.'

I want to deny it, but I cannot because he is right. I am uncomfortable. I am behaving like a small child. I choose the music today, unwilling to give him any more power in this room. I choose something I know will not be familiar to him – a Paris-based band. I had had an affair with the lead singer a few years back. It reminds me of good times, a time when I was in control.

Adam remains cool as a cucumber, and as I begin sketching I wonder what would faze him. Today I feel rage in the room. It grows as the work breaks down each and every boundary, taking from the pose exactly what it needs, the artist taking that which the girl cannot.

His body and energy tell me a story: he dislikes me; more than that he resents me, and I momentarily wonder why. What is it that this boy imagines I have done? The lines and curves on the page make pictures that I don't altogether understand, and there is darkness and rage everywhere. I had forgotten how hardcore the music of Le Petit Army is, and as Luke raps out his angry words I wonder if it is the music that has put the rage in the room or if it is coming from Adam. I channel the rage that surrounds me. He is angry and my movements become ferocious as I draw, allowing his emotions full rein on the page. The blank sheet fills up, eradicating the empty space as the images burst into life. Lots of sketches appear today, each moving into the next, almost like a cartoon strip. *Incroyable!* I have never worked like this before. And I am conscious as I continue that this is different. The artist is awake, alive. Life courses through me and I feel its vitality strongly.

My subject becomes a ball of energy, and I watch as he moves without consultation, as if I am not in the room with him. He is lost in his own thoughts, which appear on the canvas as if they are jumping from his head on to the page. It feels supernatural. As I connect with the magic, I feel Sid, his energy, a million tiny atoms gathering around me, as if Adam's rage is calling him forth. Perhaps it will protect me. I close my eyes, willing myself to connect to whatever this strangeness is, even though a part of me is afraid. I let the artist in me wrap itself around the fear and push it away. Diminished, it falls away until it is nothing more than background noise, barely noticeable while the creative symphony gathers momentum.

I sketch for hours, really listening for the first time to Luke's words as he raps about injustice. And now I write some of the words down as part of the drawings. They fit the images that have appeared, his war cries calling out to the people of France not to let their will be broken by the authorities that misgovern. Adam seems to cry out to some other authority that is in danger of breaking his spirit. My own thoughts break in. *Qu'est-ce qui vous est arrivé, Adam?* I write on the page. My eyes move from the sheet back to him, searching. Nothing comes and I realise that we are done for today but remain silent. I watch him intensely. He refuses to look my way but keeps his eyes fixed on the outside world, wanting me to know that I am insignificant to him.

'*Nous avons fini*,' I say, and he looks at me, surprised and confused for a split second, but then his expression changes to one of resentment. 'We are done,' I add.

Although I look out the window while he dresses, I see his every movement out of the corner of my eye, remembering it for later when I paint. Once he is in his clothes again, I pay him and he makes his way to the door without asking if he should come again. Perhaps we are done for good. I will know once I finish painting. But even if the work is finished I do not want him to leave my life.

'Adam?' I call out.

He turns around, his dark glasses shielding his eyes.

'Would you like to come to a concert with me?' I ask.

'Okay,' he says without a fuss.

It is unexpected. I was sure he would say no, or at least be difficult.

'It is in a nearby club tomorrow night, so perhaps you could come here first, *oui*?'

'What time?'

'Seven.'

'I'll be here.'

He turns away again and for a second time I say his name, really liking how it sounds to my ears and how it feels in my mouth. He turns towards me again.

'Thank you,' I say.

He nods and leaves.

Once he is gone I have a large mug of coffee and a few croissants, fuelling my body for a long painting session. I produce canvas after canvas, a series of events. A woman and a man appear, but there is nothing romantic about their coupling. My mind tries to understand, but I shut my thoughts down. Back I go, deep down, and the lines come and I see only shapes. I look closer and see military green – war. Battle. Pain. There is a battle between man and woman, and out of the battle comes a boy. He fights for his life, pushes his way through as she gives birth to him. And then the boy becomes the man. And the man is Adam. I stop and let go of the thought, allowing myself to step back into the abstract image where all I see is space on the page and the lines and curves that fill up that space.

Letting go of all thoughts, I continue until I finish the last picture and fall to the ground. I am exhausted, as if all my energy has gone onto the canvas. I close my eyes but I am in danger of falling into a deep sleep so I open them again. I open them and stare into a pair of angry eyes – Adam's eyes. The picture shows him naked, holding a club and ready to destroy. All around him are words that threaten vengeance. My blood runs cold.

12

Rain Dogs

I wake suddenly and see that it is 6.30 p.m. Usually it would not bother me, but today I remember that there is something happening. Of course! Adam will be here in half an hour and I have much to do. I must shower and dress. But first I must see the work. I must see all of the canvases. My dreams had been vivid green and had been of war, a continuation of my painting, and now I almost shake with anticipation as I run into the studio. I remember the feeling from yesterday, that what I was drawing was something truly amazing, and I wonder if that was true or if I was simply caught up in a self-induced euphoria. I open the door and the pictures are all there, propped up against the wall. There are twelve of them (I had thought ten, but must have miscounted). I take a step back and drop down to sit cross-legged, like a yogi about to meditate on my existence. These pictures are very powerful, almost biblical in style but with a comic-strip effect similar to the sketches I had made. It should not work, as the two different styles do not complement each other, yet it does.

The twelve paintings tell a story: a man and a woman at war and the result is a baby, birthed from a womb at knife point, and then the boy wielding a club. I remember this last picture and get the same feeling of dread as I had yesterday. The words of warning hit me again: danger is close by and I should fear for my own safety. The man and woman, clearly the parents, look suspiciously like Denzel and Alice, and the boy is most definitely Adam, his adult head sitting on the body of a child. It makes no sense, but the painting is clearly unfinished. There is more to this story, which will tell what the boy with the murderous eyes will do. We are not done yet, Adam and I.

I return to the last picture of the man-boy, destructive yet beautiful, and I am in danger of being hypnotised when the doorbell rings and pulls me away. It is 7 p.m. I know because this will be my punctual subject. I let him in and tell him to make himself a drink in the kitchen while I go and shower. He looks different and then I realise that he is travelling without his guitar, which I have come to view as part of him, like a snail carrying its shell.

I wash and dress in record time. To avoid deliberation I leave my clothing choice to fate and simply put on the first thing my hand touches in my wardrobe; it is a dress I have had forever – khaki, military style. How fitting! Finally, I dry my hair and put on some eyeliner and lipstick, wanting to look attractive, wanting Adam to find me attractive, if not beautiful. When I come out of the bedroom I find him standing at the window watching the view and drinking an orange juice.

'Have you eaten?' I ask and he nods.

I grab some juice and a bag of fresh croissants from the fridge. I pass one to him but he refuses it and continues to look outside while I eat. I finish the food quickly, partly because I am famished but mostly because I am unnerved by his silence and embarrassed by the sounds I am making as I eat. Afterwards I slip on a pair of boots, grab my coat and prepare to leave.

'Are you sure that's a good idea?' he asks when we are outside.

'I am sorry, I don't understand,' I reply.

'Maybe you should lace up your boots.'

'No, I never lace these boots. It takes too long,' I explain.

'But do you not walk out of them easily?'

'Well yes, that is precisely why I don't lace them!'

'But what if you need to run somewhere in a hurry?'

'I never run anywhere.'

'You're very spoiled,' he says and his insult hits me instantly.

'And you are very rude.'

'Yes, I am. Sorry.'

'For what you said or for being rude?'

'For being rude. I meant what I said.'

I stop walking and glare at him.

'It's true. You *are* very spoiled,' he says.

'You do not know me.'

'I think I know you a little bit – enough to know that you're spoiled.'

'Please stop saying this,' I say, my voice rising.

'Okay. Let's go,' he says.

'You know where we are going?' I am furious now. If this were anyone else I would walk away. But I still want him with me.

'Rain Dogs, isn't it?'

'Yes.'

'Well yeah, I know where we're going, then.'

I cannot be sure, but I do not remember mentioning the venue to him. The bad feeling this stubborn, awkward boy seems to prompt creeps up upon me again. I dismiss it.

We leave the complex and walk in silence. He walks faster than me and I find it difficult to keep up, but he does not slow down. Somehow I keep pace with him, worrying that at any minute I will walk out of my boots but vowing I will not. I would fall over before I would give him the satisfaction of stopping to tie my boots, as he advised. Again I get the feeling that he is punishing me and I am puzzled that I allow this, that I take what he is dishing out. I do not recognise this version of myself.

There is a queue outside the club and we stand in line for a little while. But then I hear a familiar voice at the door: Denzel has spotted us. He leads us to the front and we pass many disgruntled onlookers, resentful of our preferential treatment.

'I hope you don't mind that I brought someone,' I say when we are inside.

'No, the more the merrier,' Denzel says. 'Ah am Denzel.' He offers his hand to Adam who shakes it, which takes me by surprise – I had expected him to pull away.

Then Denzel hugs me.

'Wow! This is really impressive,' I say when I eventually take in my surroundings.

'Ja,' Denzel replies. 'That's down to Bill.' He points to the furthest corner of the room. 'You remember Bill from dinner?'

'Of course,' I say.

'Bill is my stepdad,' Denzel explains to Adam.

'Is your father here?' I ask.

'Ja, he's in the back room with Alice. They're talking to tonight's entertainment.'

A man appears behind the bar and begins singing 'Ground Control to Major Tom'. I am immediately reminded of Aqui, a bar I used to go to with Pia in Ibiza where this tune always seemed to find its way through the airwaves every time we were there. I think about Pia now, my lost friend, and I miss her.

'Hey Clive, this is Holly and this is …'

'Adam,' my date says. And he is my date, in spite of everything. I look at him and see that he has removed his dark glasses, which is the second surprise of the night – actually it is the third surprise as I think back to when he told me I was spoiled. I had hated it, even more so that he had not apologised but continued to make his point. Yes, I am spoiled. I know it, but no one other than Papa has dared tell me that before. This arrogant young man reminds me a lot of my papa and I think I am beginning to see what a young Jean-Claude Du Plessis might have been like, a young man refusing to accommodate anyone or anything, much like I had been before I started accommodating this arrogant Adam.

'Ja, Adam,' Denzel says and smiles his huge smile. 'Clive will make you a drink and then we can take a seat at the front table in the middle. Ah've reserved it for us all – the best seat in the house. Just pull up another chair for Adam. Ah'm pleased to know you, boet.'

Adam nods but doesn't say anything. He seems to be a little intimidated by Denzel, or maybe that is wishful thinking on my part. I would like nothing more than to see him intimidated in the same way that he intimidates me.

We get some drinks and sit in silence while the club fills up around us. I feel very awkward but cannot find any signs that my companion is suffering in the same way. Eventually I go to the bathroom, not because I need to but because I want to get away – and because I want to see myself in the mirror. I am disgusted at my own vanity, but I actually want to check how I look; Adam does not seem to see anything worth looking at on my face. Alone, I study myself in the mirror and decide that I look good. But why can he not see this? The dress hugs me in the places it should, but he had only commented on my boots and my open laces. I feel more self-conscious than I can ever remember feeling before. Here in this tiny room sorrow catches up with me and I begin to cry, huge sobs that I stifle with my hands, cursing myself for falling apart now when I am out in company. *Non, ma chérie,* be strong, I tell myself. *Serrer les dents,* my papa would say if he were here. And so I do my best and eventually manage to pull myself together.

When I get back to the table, Tim, Bill and Alice have joined Adam. The only other woman at our table is talking to the boy I want so desperately to like me. He seems to be enjoying himself and I am instantly jealous. This was maybe how she felt the last time we met when she watched me talking to Denzel.

'Hello Holly,' she says and embraces me at arm's length, as if I might infect her with something. 'Adam has just been telling us that he's newly arrived from Dublin.'

I nod and realise that in a few short minutes he has given them more than he has given me in the last three days.

'How have you been, Holly?' Bill asks.

'I am good,' I say. 'Painting lots.'

'Wonderful,' he says, and then Denzel introduces the musician and everyone's attention moves to the stage.

As I sit listening, I am conscious of Adam all the time. Try as I might I cannot seem to switch off his imposing presence. My work with him is not finished, so I will need to spend more time with him, but after that I decide I will back away. I must; this boy is clearly not good for me. No one has ever made me feel this bad about myself, and that cannot be a good thing. I have firmly made up my mind and am just beginning to enjoy the comfort the decision brings me when I feel his leg leaning against mine. He lets it stay there, and I allow myself to be swept along by the magnetism of his energy.

It is an intense feeling and I realise that, despite the fact that I have spent the best part of three afternoons with him and seen him naked, this is the first time we have touched. It is electric, and for the first time I begin to think that whatever game this boy is playing, he feels the same connection between us as I do. In spite of myself and the internal alarm bell that begins to ring loudly, I take hold of his hand.

13

Adam's Eyes: Part II

I take the hand offered and, although this is a huge moment, nothing happens – no thunder bolts or lightning. For the first time, I am directly connecting with my father. I have played this moment over in my head a thousand times, making it into this huge, dramatic event, but in reality it is nothing – less than nothing – and the great rage is nowhere. I am numb to my surroundings. They embrace, he and Holly, and I can sense something, an attraction between the two. He wants her. Pretty Alice is not enough for him, dirty bastard!

He leaves, taking my attention with him. I watch him, every inch of him, as he walks off. Holly gets us drinks, just as it should be, and I wait, happy that she is feeling how she is feeling. Gone is the full-of-herself girl that I first met, replaced by a pathetic, desperate creature that I like more. I have done this to her; the thought alone makes me smile.

Holly returns to the table and I deliberately don't thank her; it is not in my nature to be bad-mannered but I remind myself that she deserves it. This girl is privileged, and spoiled. How she had hated it when I said that! I bet she has never known hardship. Or rejection. Now she is probably wondering why I am treating her this way, what might be wrong with her. I hope so. Someone else should feel how I feel – wrong on the inside.

I watch as Denzel Anderson leaves and goes behind the stage. I think about following him and telling him who I am, now, on this night, when he is oblivious to everything else, except maybe Holly. He'd noticed her all right. He's probably fantasising about taking her outside and giving her a good seeing to, just like he did with Marie Sheehan. Fucking prick!

A voice bursts into my thoughts and I hear a David Bowie song about someone called Major Tom trying to reach ground control. The voice isn't bad actually. It belongs to the barman who I've just been introduced to. He sits beside me.

'Hey mate,' he says. 'How goes it?'

'Grand,' I tell him, wanting to sound Irish for some reason. I've noticed that I want to sound different in this foreign country, I want to sound Irish. It seems I have deep roots. They must have grown while I was busy not caring.

'You finding your way around okay?' he asks.

'I think so,' I reply.

'London's a hard place when you first get here. I've never been to Dublin. Imagine that! Even though my mother is from there and we've family there who've managed to come over here. But none of us have ever gone there. Isn't that incredible?'

'Yeah,' I say, but I don't think it's that incredible. If I lived in London I wouldn't bother going to Dublin. I haven't been here long but it seems to be the same as Dublin, only on a larger scale and with more to offer.

'It's on my list of things to do. And I'd like to take my son there,' says Clive.

'You have a son?' I ask, in spite of myself, curiosity getting the better of me. This man doesn't look like someone who should have a family.

'Yep. He's called Ben and he's a little cracker. He lives with his mother and her husband, but I have him every other weekend.'

So he doesn't have a family, not really.

'What age is he?' I ask.

'He's five and growing up to be a smashing little boy. Alice used to teach him, actually. Denzel's wife. Yeah, she taught my son before she ever knew me. Before she and Denzel got together. It's a small world. You know the story, right?'

I shake my head.

'Okay, I'll leave it at that, then,' he says, and I don't object, even though I wish he'd tell me more.

'So what's your story?' he asks, but I don't get a chance to answer as the rest of the people joining us at our table arrive.

'Everyone, this is Adam,' Denzel says.

Names are thrown my way and hands are offered. My grandfather is the last and the most reluctant. He looks at me but doesn't really take me in. Why should he! Another arrogant artist! Alice sits beside me and I get goosebumps, as if the temperature around me has dropped. Her resemblance to Marie, my mother, is uncanny.

'Where's Holly?' she asks.

'She's in the bathroom,' I reply, working hard to sound normal even though I feel anything but.

'The place I spend so much of my time these days,' she says, rubbing her belly. I look at the bump in front of her and it hits me: she is carrying my half-brother or sister in there. My heartstrings draw closer.

'You're Irish,' she says and I nod. 'I went to Dublin once and loved it so much. It's a lot like London – well, a mini London – but the people are very different. I liked the people.'

'I'm from Dublin,' I tell her. I like this woman, in spite of everything. Although she looks like Marie she is nothing like her. This woman is warm and kind, unlike the others. I feel sorry for her and wonder what bad thing she's done that life has put her with my asshole father.

Holly comes back just as the music is about to begin. She waves to everyone before sitting beside me and I see her cheeks redden. She's embarrassed. I can feel Alice watching us, wanting to know what's going on, and so I give her and my father something to look at: I set my knee against Holly's. It is the first time I have touched her and I can sense her reaction. She is shaking slightly and it reminds me of Aoife Fitzpatrick. I had done the exact same thing to her and a few hours later we were in her bedroom.

Aoife was one of the girls at my school, silly and desperate for some attention. She fancied me and would go all red in the face whenever she spoke to me. After Mammy died I missed school, and Aoife kept notes for me and said that if I ever needed to talk she was there. I thought that was sweet but I didn't take her up on her offer. The poor girl hadn't a clue, really, no more than I did before Mammy got sick. I was nice to her though. It wasn't her fault that she was young and naïve, wanting what all the girls her age wanted, one of us boys to pay her some attention.

I had sex with her the night after I found out everything, when Bernie had been unable to find any words that could make me feel better. In fairness, what could she have said? What could anyone have said? The sex with Aoife would probably never have happened if I hadn't just discovered that I was the product of rape. But I had and it did.

Up until that night I'd been a virgin. I was saving myself. For what, I didn't really know. When I told her I was a virgin she looked like I had given her the keys to her first house. She caught hold of my erection, the first girl I'd ever let do that, and it felt good. She knew what she was doing, had johnnies and everything, and slipped one on me like an old pro. I came quickly the first time, but then we had another go and this time I lasted much longer. It was easy really, and we'd got better and better at it over the next six months. Up until I left, without a word. We weren't going out together – she knew the score and said she didn't mind. It was our secret; it made her want it more. But to be honest, I just took whatever was going and enjoyed it, but I could easily have done without it. Unlike my father. Fucking animal!

I watch him now as he caresses Alice's stomach like he's some sort of saint and again I feel sorry for her. If she had the full measure of him she'd push his dirty hand away from her unborn child. No longer feeling numb, my fury bubbles up to the surface and I embrace it, finding a comfort in it. I turn my attention to Holly and am just about to move my leg, which doesn't appear to be having the same effect on her as it did on Aoife, when she takes hold of my hand. I don't pull away, knowing that I'm on my way to another girl's bedroom in the near future.

14

An Unexpected Visitor

I look at the naked body beside me. Raphael has come to London, and following a night-time visit he is in my bed. It is a happy distraction and the kind of attention I need so much right now, not to mention the sex, which has always been great. We know each other's bodies well, what we like and what we do not like. Last night Adam had left me confused. He had definitely made an advance in the club, but afterwards he had simply walked away and left me to come home alone. Hurt and confused, I had walked around the nearby park, a very dangerous thing to do but I did not care – I was inviting danger. And then Raphael had called to tell me he was in London, heaven-sent to look after me.

And yet I think of Adam now as I lie with Raphael. And I want Adam. Even sex with Raphael has not stopped my longing. I want most what I cannot have perhaps, but it feels like it is something more akin to what Sid Harris had opened me up to: the possibility of something deeper. Raphael wakes up and kisses my forehead.

'Right, I will cook breakfast,' he says and gets up.

Yes, having him around has its advantages. I do some cat stretches in the bed before I join him in the kitchen.

'I was thinking I might stay in London for a while with you. Would that be okay?' he asks.

'Yes, that could work,' I say, glad of the company and hoping that perhaps if Adam sees there is someone else in my life he will become interested. Men are often like that, wanting what belongs to another.

'You are painting here?' Raphael asks.

'Yes, and I have found a subject.'

'Already? Is it the man from Ibiza?'

'No. Someone I met here, actually.'

'How do you mean, you met them here?'

'I met him in a coffee shop. He was busking outside and I noticed him.'

'Holly, you are a danger to yourself, you know! A complete stranger! And you've had him here!'

'Calm down, Raphael. It is fine.'

'No, it is not fine. I worry about you.'

'Why? I never understand why.'

'No, you don't.' He looks at me with big sad eyes, reminding me of the real issue I choose to ignore. I should break my connection with Raphael and let him get on with his life. But selfishly I don't because I need him – and his cooking skills.

'Croque-monsieur – my favourite!' I exclaim.

'Of course!' he replies.

'Thank you so much,' I say and he nods.

We sit and eat, looking out at the great view.

'I have always loved this place,' he says.

'Me too. And Papa.'

'Where is he now?'

'New York. But he may come visit soon.'

'Ah yes, he has an exhibition at the Guggenheim soon.'

I nod.

'He is working still?'

'Yes. How long do you want to stay, Raphael?'

'A few weeks. I have a show in Amsterdam in a few months and I would like to get there in advance to set up. You could come when I am there, if you like.'

'Maybe. It is a while since I have been to Amsterdam. What is the show?'

'Some pictures I took last year at the major fashion shows.'

I nod. 'Why do you not find yourself a model, Raphael? You spend so much time with those beautiful creatures and yet you are here with me.'

'You know why, Holly. Do not do this. It is cruel!'

'I'm sorry, Raphael. I don't mean to be cruel. Really.'

The intercom buzzes and surprises us both.

'Are you expecting company?' he asks.

I shake my head. 'Perhaps Papa is here.'

I begin to stand up, but Raphael motions for me to stay and goes out to the hallway.

'It is Adam,' he says, sticking his head back in through the door. 'Yes or no?'

'Yes,' I reply.

I am shocked, but I am also excited. Raphael goes back to the intercom and buzzes him in. Then we wait, Raphael beside me like a watch dog. When Adam eventually appears he does not look at all affected by the presence of this stranger.

'Hello,' he says simply.

'Hello,' I reply.

I do not introduce Raphael and Adam. I do not want to give Adam anything more. It will be obvious that Raphael and I have spent the night together. That's all I want him to know.

'I thought we were meeting today,' Adam says.

'No, tomorrow. But now that you are here we might as well work,' I say.

'Okay,' he replies.

'I'm Adam,' he says, turning his attention to Raphael.

'Raphael.'

'Go into the studio and I will be there in a little while. I just need to finish my brunch and get changed,' I say.

Adam walks into the studio and closes the door behind him.

'Strange boy,' Raphael says. 'Honestly, Holly!'

I do not respond but merely go back to my food and drink my coffee. Then I go to change.

'You're still painting half-naked?' Raphael snaps when I pass him on my way to the studio.

'Since when did you become the priest,' I say and leave him to it.

Inside the studio I find Adam naked, and I am surprised as well as aroused. I begin to sketch, today in silence – somehow it is what I need. As I draw, I feel as if I can climb easily inside his head now. He wants to know who this Raphael is but will not ask. I feel it and, in addition, I feel something else today. My longing is not one-sided. Finally, he wants me.

He had come here to fuck me and now I notice that he is aroused too. I let my eyes linger between his legs. I have a strong urge to take him now. My nipples are hard and I touch one, enjoying the feeling and waiting for him to look my way. But he does not. Instead, he takes hold of himself and begins to masturbate silently. I watch for a short time without moving a muscle, no longer painting but suspended in the sexual tension that has taken over the room. I accept its invitation and slip my hand under my t-shirt to catch hold of my breast. I place my foot on the window ledge so that I have access to my own sexual centre. I touch myself and am not surprised to find that I am wet, as if I have just stepped out of some water. I gasp as I feel the pressure from my own fingers and I caress myself as I watch him. Adam continues to pleasure himself as if I am not in the room. His face is turned towards the window, but I can see that his eyes are closed. He is keeping the experience to himself, excluding me. However, his body sends out an invitation to watch, and I take in all the subtle movements as it reacts to his stimulation. It is so arousing. However, it is his face that hooks me as I watch expressions pass across it that I have not seen before. It is both pleasure and pain rolled into one, suffering and ecstasy within the one moment, and I watch carefully, recording it with my inner eye so I might paint it later. I become more aroused and can hear my breathing get louder; my body craves swifter movement. My hand obliges and my hips begin to move, and I do not care any more, even when Adam climaxes and opens his eyes to watch me. As he does I climax too, a slow, hard, silent orgasm. He watches with satisfaction on his face. This is his victory.

He walks towards me, and I wonder what is about to happen. This feels all wrong with Raphael in the other room. But my guilt is only fleeting; if he were to take me now I would let him. I would not be able to resist. As it turns out I do not need to consider this, for he walks past me to the bin to discard the tissue that he had ejaculated into. The moment collapses, well and truly. He begins dressing. Today he decides when we finish. He is in control now. But of course he has always been in control, and I get a feeling that what just happened was about letting me know that. When he is dressed he waits, and I wonder why until he glances towards my purse on the table, reminding me of our business arrangement.

I pay him with the hand that is covered in my scent, and he looks me straight in the eye as he takes it, letting his hand linger on mine. I feel the same charge that I had felt in the club when we held hands, and I search for evidence that he feels it too. *Mon Dieu,* he must! The feelings between us are unbelievably intense and I think of Sid now, although this is not like it had been with my beautiful English boy. There is no tenderness here – just raw attraction that has a sharp edge to it, feeling like it might physically cut through me, slicing my most intimate parts.

'Who is he?' he asks.

'Nobody,' I say.

His eyes fill with something that looks like repulsion and I realise what I have just said and how it must sound: cold and bitchy. And spoiled. I am the rich, spoilt girl he had accused me of being.

'I mean he is just a friend. But not a ...' I realise I am making it worse, so I stop talking.

'See you tomorrow,' he says and leaves me alone among his sketches.

He is gone, yet I am covered with him and a longing for something in this boy that might not exist. But still I will search just in case, because if it is possible that I might find that wonderful love I had once with Sid, it will be worth all my efforts.

15

Ultimatum

Raphael is nowhere to be seen. I am alone, thinking, wondering what does it all mean? What are we doing, this boy and I? I have finished painting for today; the story is to be continued. Today, in my story, boy met girl and I suspect the girl is me, that I have completed a few self-portraits. It will be a first time for me, outside of when I was studying and made to do it. My work is evolving.

It is late. I had painted for a long time, and Raphael got sick and tired of waiting and left. Now I wonder where he is. I could call him and find out, but I don't. I let him be out there, away from me. He had been upset by the appearance of Adam and had guessed something was up by my reaction. Whether I like it or not, Raphael knows me better than anyone else in the world. Sid knew me in a deeper way, but Raphael has known me the longest.

I hear the front door downstairs open just as I am thinking about going to bed. A little time later a drunk Raphael appears in the doorway of the apartment.

'I will leave now,' he says.

'*Pourquoi*?'

'I have had enough, Holly!'

'What do you mean?'

'I can't do this any more. I want something more from you and it is not possible that I will get it. I can't hang around waiting any longer. It is not good for either of us.'

'But Raphael, you are my friend!'

'No, I am not your friend. I am someone you use. Let us be honest. You have been using me since we first met. Since I first saw you in Jean-Claude's studio in Paris I have been almost possessed. You were no more than a girl, so I waited until you showed an interest. I knew it was the older man thing that attracted you. You wanted someone to teach you how to love physically, and I taught you well. But for me it is much more than that – always has been. I love you, Holly, but you are unable to return my feelings. So it is best I don't see you.'

'So you are saying you will not even be my friend?'

'*C'est impossible* – I cannot! Don't you see! You broke my heart in Ibiza, telling me you were in love with someone else. And when he died I thought – well, I'm not sure exactly what I thought, but I expected more than what this last year has brought. But this Adam – it is too much! I saw you with him. He is a little young, don't you think? He is only a boy. You flaunt your flings in front of me and I can't take it any more.'

'But there is nothing going on between me and the boy,' I protest, but my face turns bright red, giving me away.

He shakes his head. 'I don't know if you are lying just to me or also to yourself. I am not blind, Holly. So no more! There is a girl in Milan.'

'That is great!' I say, trying to sound a lot happier than I feel about this news. I do not want him, yet I do not want anyone else to have him. Shame on me!

'No, it is not great! The girl in Milan has been there all along and she loves me, yet I keep coming back to you. She knows about you and tells me that I am a fool for giving so much to someone who cares nothing for me, and she is right.'

'But I do care for you, Raphael! You must know that! You are the best friend I have.'

'You do not treat me like a best friend. Come on! Not even you can believe that.'

Again I turn bright red. All he is saying is true. I have taken advantage of his love for me. 'You are right,' I say. 'I am sorry, Raphael.' Tears pour down my cheeks as I begin to feel remorse for my actions and sorrow that I will lose him. He sits beside me on the sofa and puts his arm around me.

'Do you remember when Ari died?' I ask.

He nods. The day Ari died was the day that Raphael and I first got together. I knew he had feelings for me, and that night I had taken full advantage, wanting to eradicate the awful numbness that had settled after hearing the devastating news. We had sex and Raphael took my virginity, professing his love for me. But for me it was not about love, it was about loss.

'I would not have coped if I had not known you then,' I continue. 'You were there for me, and since then there have been so many times you have been there for me, Raphael. I do love you. You must know that.'

'Could you imagine spending the rest of your life with me? Marrying me? Giving me children?'

I bite my trembling lower lip. I want to tell him that perhaps I can change, but I don't because I know it would be ludicrously unfair. If he is not enough now then it is likely that he will never be enough.

'No, Raphael, you are right. But can you not stay my friend? I need you in my life.'

'But that is just it Holly – you need me, but I do not need you. You are not good for me.'

His words sting me.

'I want to try with this girl from Milan, but the only way I can do it is to be away from you. Do you understand?'

I nod.

'But not for forever – just for a little time, *oui*?' I ask.

'I don't know. It is best that you don't contact me, I think. Just let me be.'

I am sobbing now and he puts his arms around me. I remember the first time he did it. It was this emotion that had brought him close to me and made me want him. The same thing had happened after Sid, when I returned to Paris and called him and as always he had come. And now I want the same thing – rough sex tangled up with a sorrow that feels raw and inaccessible. When he is inside me he seems to touch the heart of it and pound it out of me.

I grab hold of him, wrapping my legs around him and kissing him hungrily, and I feel him reacting. He finds the condom pack easily, and we move from the settee to the floor where we can roll about wildly, trying to find the best positions that allow him to enter me deeply. He pulls out of me, letting me know that he wants me another way, and experience tells me what to do. I get on all fours and he enters me from behind. I push my face into the cold wall, my head banging against the hard surface as he slaps up against me until I orgasm with such intensity that my legs go from under me. We tumble to the floor and he rolls me over. He finds me still orgasming and thrusts his huge erection inside me, causing me to cry out as my climax intensifies and leads into another and another. Finally, he joins me and we are both left gasping and moaning.

'Are you sure you want to stop this?' I ask when I can eventually speak again.

'Still you don't understand!' he says and stands up. 'But you never did, that is the problem. I don't want to stop this. But for my own sanity I have to! Every time we do this I get hurt.'

I nod. I do understand really. As I think about Raphael I come back to dwell on the situation with Adam and I feel the same fear as before. Yes, I understand, Raphael, and I think that pretty soon I will be standing in your shoes wanting this angry stranger who seems to have crawled under my skin. Although the sex with Raphael has extinguished one level of desire, there is a whole other pocket of longing deeper inside of me, longing that I sense can only be taken away by this intense boy.

'I am sorry, Raphael,' I tell him and kiss him softly on the lips.

He cups my face in his hands. '*Moi aussi*,' he says.

He begins to get dressed and I realise that he is preparing to leave.

'You are going now? *Mon Dieu*, stay until the morning at least!'

He shakes his head. 'It is best I go now and take the first flight out of here.'

'To Amsterdam?'

'No, to Milan. To Natalia.'

'That is a lovely name.'

'She is a lovely girl. And if it weren't for you she would be enough.' He looks at me with his big sad eyes, making me feel tremendously guilty.

'I never meant for it to be like this, Raphael. I wish it could be different,' I tell him.

'I know. But it does not help.'

He looks at me for a long time as if he is committing me to memory and my eyes begin to fill with tears again.

'I remember when you were a young girl I could see the woman you would become and I watched you grow into her. You are the most beautiful woman I have ever known. But there is no point in loving you. It is a waste of everybody's time.'

I want to say something but I can think of nothing to say. It is a lost cause. Papa is right; to expect life to be fair is ridiculous. Raphael finishes packing and I start to get dressed, but he stops me.

'No, do not come to the door. You stay here.'

'I will miss you,' I say and my voice breaks.

'I know. I will miss you too.' He reaches the apartment door and stops. 'This Adam,' he says, keeping his back to me. 'Be careful. There is something not right with him.'

I do not answer and watch as my safety net walks away.

16
A Walk In The Park

I wake up to an empty bed and immediately feel low. A relationship of over fifteen years is over. Just like that, Raphael is no longer in my life. Another kind of death. I wonder if I have made a big mistake. Perhaps I could try to make it work with him? Maybe I would surprise myself. I am close to calling him and begging him to come back, but I cannot go through with it. He has his girl in Milan and perhaps he can make that work. If I am truly his friend I would want that for him. Yes, to take him away from the possibility of love just because I am afraid to be without him would be cruel and unforgivable. If he has the chance of happiness I should not stand in the way. I have been unfair to him in the past, but now is my chance to make up for it.

Once the cloak of sleepiness has fully lifted, I make my way to the studio and habitual behaviour takes over. The images that stare back at me burst forth and are very powerful. Two people, me and Adam. But it is not love. It is something else. Lust? Or maybe obsession. And there is rage rather than tenderness behind the passion. The pictures are devoid of tenderness. It tells me much about myself. These days it feels as if the tenderness in me has gone. Sid had been the most tender man I had ever known, and it touched those parts deep inside me. After he died it felt as if it had stayed with me for a time, leaving me exposed and vulnerable. But it seems to have disappeared again. It is certainly nowhere in these pictures. Neither had it been present when Raphael and I fucked for what was probably the last time. Our coupling had never been tender, yet my experience of love with Sid was that it awakens that which is tender. No, I don't believe Raphael loves me, just as he does not believe me to be his friend. He is right. It is for the best that we part. Although I will miss him the loss I feel is different to that sense of loss I have for Sid. Raphael is still in this world should I need him; Sid is gone forever.

Looking at my paintings I see the green shades that are everywhere in this room. But now they are less dark. Perhaps the light is coming through. As I look at the pictures, I realise that today is not a day for painting; it is a day to be outside. So when Adam arrives I suggest that we walk, and he agrees, after reminding me that he is on my payroll no matter what we do. I pay him without a word.

We head for the Tower of London in silence. The strangeness is still between us after yesterday's episode in the studio. As we walk, my thoughts race. I think about what happened between us, realising that I don't know how to process it because I am not sure what 'it' was. We have been together sexually but as if the other were not in the room. Why am I surprised that it is strange; nothing in our connection has been typical or comfortable.

'He's gone,' Adam says, pulling me out of my thoughts.

I nod.

'He couldn't handle it.'

'What do you mean?' I ask defensively.

'He couldn't handle you.'

'Why are you like this, Adam?' I ask.

He shrugs. 'I dislike you,' he says eventually and I am shocked by his admission.

'Wow, you are too honest,' I say before I can stop myself.

He laughs as if we are in the playground and he has just pulled my hair. 'For you, maybe!' he says and rolls his eyes.

'*Mon Dieu*! What age are you, Adam!' I say, wanting to find a way to humiliate him.

'Does it matter?' he replies.

'You act like the child sometimes! You are very young.'

'That depends on the measure you are using.'

I look at him and he smiles, diffusing my anger.

'That is the first time you have smiled at me,' I say.

'Probably. I don't smile a lot, so don't take it personally.'

'But I do. You are nasty to me!' I say, immediately regretting how it sounds. 'You are very weird.'

'You can talk!' he scoffs and again I feel like we are in the playground.

'I suppose that is true. My work has taken a new direction with you as my subject.'

'*Your subject*! God, you're so pretentious,' he says bitterly.

I blush and look away so he will not see. 'Have you ever masturbated in front of somebody before?' I ask, hoping to put him into a state of unease just as he has done with me.

'No, have you?' he replies.

'No.' It is a lie.

'I enjoyed it,' he says.

'Me too,' I reply, and get an urge to catch hold of his hand but I do not. It is up to him.

'Could we do it again?' he asks and again he sounds like a little boy.

'Yes,' I reply.

We stop by a bench and sit down without any need to consult each other. Our view is of lush green trees and a scattering of people. Not alone yet somehow alone, the silence rests with us and thoughts begin to swirl in my head as I sit with this mysterious boy. I have never had sex with a subject while I was painting them. Quite often I would afterwards, but never before or during. It is a rule of mine but one that I am in danger of breaking. The truth is that if Adam were to try something now I would go with it, for the foreplay has already started and I am in a state. His ill treatment is seductive and arousing and it makes me want him and the danger attached to him.

'You said you dislike me, Adam. But the thing is I really like you, and I am not sure why to be honest!' It blurts out so suddenly that I wonder if someone else might have said it. Perhaps his blatant honesty is contagious.

He does not respond, leaving me hanging in the knowledge that I have changed everything. From now on, we are heading in one direction. For good or bad, the events of the future have been set in motion.

Eventually we stand up, again without a word and almost in sync, and then to my complete surprise Adam takes my hand as if it is a perfectly normal thing to do. We walk back to the apartment in silence, and I swear I can feel a connection establish itself as our linked limbs enable the charge to flow freely between us. Yes, there is most definitely chemistry, and even his continual bad behaviour cannot persuade me otherwise.

At the door to the apartment I stand and wait to see what he suggests next. He looks at me with his navy-blue eyes for what feels like a long time. Is he trying to decide whether or not to come inside? If he does we both know what will happen. I watch and wait. The possibility flickers in his eyes and the window of opportunity begins to open, but then something in him shuts it down again. I can almost see it as it happens.

'Should I come at two tomorrow?' he asks, his words deflating the tension.

'Yes,' I say and turn to go inside.

Adam takes hold of me and, turning me back towards him, kisses me on the lips. A single kiss that stretches time beyond the few seconds it lasts.

Then he leaves me without a word, as if it had never happened. I am unable to move for a while. I bring my hand to my lips as if to check that they are still there, that he hasn't taken them with him.

Adam walks out of sight and I am alone. I search my pockets for my keys, open the door and prepare to shut off the alarm, which mostly I forget about but today I had set because I was feeling on edge knowing I would walk with Adam. But it does not sound. And then I hear him call my name. Papa is home.

17
Talking Love

'What is going on, Holly?' Papa asks me. We are talking in English so I guess he is still in New York mode.

'What do you mean?'

'Well, you leave Paris just like that, and Bebe calls me and says you are not acting like yourself. She is worried.'

Bebe, my surrogate mother since my biological mother relinquished any responsibility for my upbringing, has become my real mother over the years and continually worries about me.

'She told me to get on a plane and find out what was up, and so here I am,' says Papa.

I cannot help but smile at their anxieties. If ever I doubt that I am loved I only need to think of these two people.

'But I told you I came here to work, Papa! We spoke on the phone and I told you!'

'Yes, we spoke about the work but not about you. So, young lady, what is going on with you. Tell me. Now.'

'I don't know, Papa. I guess I am still grieving.'

'But it has been over a year, *non*? Time to move on.'

'But it is not that simple. I loved him.'

'If that is true you should be happy and moving on, not sitting pining for someone who is no longer here.'

'That is not what I am doing.'

'Bebe thinks it is.'

'Well, she is wrong.'

'It is not like Bebe to be wrong. In all the years I have known her she always gets these things right. She is seldom wrong.'

'But seldom is not never, and now she is wrong.'

'So my plane journey was wasted.'

'Yes,' I say, and then I begin to cry.

Papa pours me a stiff brandy and hands it to me. 'Have this, *chérie*. It will help. And then tell me everything.'

I take a few sips and begin to speak as if I have just drank a truth serum. 'I miss him Papa and I don't know what to do with that. You do not understand because you have never felt like this about anyone. You have never really loved. But I have. And then Raphael came to stay but left yesterday, saying we cannot be friends any more because I don't love him like he loves me. There is a girl in Milan who loves him. And then I met this boy over here who is very mean to me … and it is all too much.' I realise, almost too late, that I do not want to talk about Adam.

'So you think your papa has never loved, and yet I am here?' he says.

'You know what I mean. Love is "for the birds", as you say.'

'And this is precisely why I say it. How can this be a good thing if it makes you feel so bad?'

'But it was the best thing. To really love someone and to want to share everything with them, every little moment, your whole life.'

'Don't I do that with you, my family, my flesh and blood? You are made of the same stuff as me. I didn't choose to make you, yet you are here, and we are connected by blood. It is different, and it is only possible to love in this way the people that blood connects you to. The rest is a farce. Women and men should come together to make little beings and then get on with it. All of this fascination with romantic love is a waste of time. A fantasy. There are two sexes so that reproduction can happen and the next generation can be produced. That is our sole purpose. Sex partners are not linked to each other, and to expect the same sort of loyalty and commitment from someone who is a stranger, from someone who is not blood, is ludicrous. The human psyche does not work like that. I mean look at the animal world. They understand this.'

'No, Papa, I disagree! I felt something for Sid as if he was my family. We were connected by something else and we were able to share things, to think about building a life together.'

'But how can you say that! You knew him only five minutes. Love is for life.'

'You are cruel, Papa!' I shout. I am angry as only Papa can make me, telling me things I don't want to hear or believe, telling me in a way that might make them true. I hate it.

'*Non. Non. Non. Non!*' I say. I all but stamp my feet.

Papa smiles at me.

'Don't get angry, please. It is the truth I tell you, as I always do. I have no intention of hurting you, *chérie*. It would be the same as hurting myself, *non*? This love is for the birds.'

'Please stop saying that and accept for one minute the possibility that you might just be wrong,' I say. 'You always tell me not to be so stubborn that I cannot see my own shortcomings. I say the same to you now.'

'Ah, so the child wants to teach the parent something. Good! Okay, so let us say this love exists, just for argument's sake. Does it make you feel happy now?'

'No, but it did.'

'That is not what I asked, Holly. It does not make you happy now, so is it love? Isn't love meant to nourish and feed us and make us happy to be alive? This is making you sad and angry and irrational, which is what it does to everyone, in my experience, and I live from my own experience, not what others tell me.'

'*Touché!*'

He laughs. 'I raised too clever a child.'

'You have never felt it? Honestly?'

'Yes! I feel love with you, and with Bebe. It is extraordinary. It is the glue that holds me together.'

'Ah, but Bebe is not flesh and blood.'

'But, *chérie*, of course she is! She is my half-sister.'

I look at my father, shocked.

'Papa! Why have you never told me before?'

'Okay, I have let the cat out of the bag, but you cannot tell Bebe I told you. She is very proud and it would break her heart to know that I betrayed her, even to you. Bebe was the daughter of my father and a local woman who was below his station. She was raised as a bastard and there was great shame in that, so she forgot as soon as she could – as soon as life gave her the opportunity.'

'How did you find her?'

'My father told me about her when he was dying and I tracked her down afterwards. I asked her to come to Paris with me and she agreed, but only if I promised not to tell anyone of our "shameful" connection. So she came to work for me.'

'*Mon Dieu*! Bebe is my aunt!'

'Bebe is your mother, Holly. *Non*? But yes, she is our flesh and blood.'

'You should have told me!'

'And betray my only other living relative? I know I have done it now, but it is for a good cause. You must not tell her you know, Holly. It is a very shameful thing for Bebe. Her good name and social standing are the most important things to her. You understand, *oui*?'

'Yes. It makes sense. I often wondered why you did not marry her.'

'Well, now you know why, but promise me, Holly.'

'I promise,' I say. 'But I still think you are wrong.'

'Okay, *chérie*, but you should listen to your own advice and accept the possibility that *you* might just be wrong.'

'Okay.' I laugh, not able to stay mad any more.

He puts his hand on my shoulder. 'It will all be fine, *chérie*. It always is in the end. That is something life teaches you. The times when things seem all mixed up are just intermissions between the times of clarity, making us appreciate them more, *oui*?'

'*Oui.*'

He hugs me. 'I am glad I came. I was worried, but I had another reason for coming to see you. I was curious about this work. I wanted to see your paintings. I am afraid my impatience got the better of me and I went to the studio to see. You have gone all biblical!'

'Yes, it does have a religious feel,' I say.

'You are telling the story of Adam and Eve. *Non*? The apple, the couple, the birth of Cain, the boy born out of sin. But where is Abel?'

I begin to laugh. Of course! I hadn't seen it before!

'There is something funny?'

'Yes, Papa. I hadn't noticed that, but when you point it out it is obvious.'

'It is very beautiful work – and such magnificent greens.'

'Thank you!' My heart swells in my chest.

'So tell me of this boy who is torturing you?'

This is a conversation I do not want to have with my papa, but it is pointless telling him that because he will talk anyway.

'Oh, it is nothing. I wish I had never mentioned it!'

'It does not sound like nothing. Who is he?'

'Just a boy I met over here.'

'Where did you meet him?'

'In a coffee shop.'

'So you have no idea who he is? Or his background?'

'No.'

'Mmmm. And what is the matter with him?'

'I don't know. He is sometimes cruel. He tells me that I am spoiled.'

'But you are *chérie*.' He smiles at me.

'But only you are allowed to say that to me,' I say.

'And what else?'

'I don't know. He is just cruel.' My face starts to redden.

'Could it be that he is not under your spell, like so many men have been?'

My papa, always hitting the nail on the head and I hate it. I feel the anger rise in me again. He is right, of course. He tells me the plain facts without dressing them up or sugar-coating his words. Harsh reality is what my papa always speaks of. Anything other than that is a waste of time in his books. I used to respect that about him, but now I am not so sure. I want a little fantasy, a few dreams. What is wrong with creating our own worlds! *Mon Dieu*, enough people do it! But no, today we are speaking the truth, and if Papa wants to talk truth perhaps I should do the same.

'That is part of it. I agree. But there is something else. I think he has a problem with women. He thinks badly of them, like they are playthings and not to be trusted.'

'Like me.'

'Yes.'

'Perhaps you have met your father. If you have I would advise you to move on to the next man. This love for the birds is only possible with men who are not like me. If romance is what you really want then do not push for it with him. That would be torture. *Non*?'

I shrug.

'You say that Raphael and you are no longer friends. How can this be?'

'He wants us to be together but I don't.'

'Would it be so terrible?'

'Yes! I cannot give him what he wants. I cannot love him like he wants me to love him.'

'But perhaps he is happy to take only what you can give?'

'It does not work that way, Papa!'

'For lots of people it does. Raphael is a good man and he is your best friend. I think you could be very good for each other. I have known him and his family a long time and they are good people. I have watched him love you over the years and it has not diminished, no matter what you do. There are not many people who could be like that with you, you know that, don't you? I think you are making a mistake, Holly, because you are fantasising about your Sid, the kind of relationship that might only have been in your head.'

'I am shocked, Papa!'

'Why?'

'That you can say this, you think this. It is unfair and not helpful.'

'But I think it is very helpful. I wish someone had been there to stop me making the mistakes I made.'

'Like meeting my mother?'

'*Chérie*, are you the teenager all over again? Why do you say that?'

Now the anger comes to the surface, flaring up. Papa does this to me like no one else can. 'Don't patronise me, Jean-Claude! You do not know how it was for me, living with you all those years and growing up while you chased after girls my age. Do you know how that made me feel – my father fucking every young woman in sight like they were dispensable, things to be used and then disposed of? What kind of message did that send to me about being a woman – or about men, for that matter? Did you ever think about that while you lived as if you were without any responsibilities? You disgusted me back then, and when I think about it now, it still disgusts me!'

I stop talking, shocked by my own words, and I look at my father's face. He seems hurt, but there is something else in his eyes that I have never seen before. I wait for him to speak but he does not.

'I am sorry,' I say eventually.

He nods and tells me it is okay, but I know it is not. The man who always promised to tell me the truth and who has mostly managed to live by that promise has just told me a lie.

18
Sowing The Seed

The door buzzes at 2 p.m. as usual, and I open it to find Adam standing there. Today he hands me something.

'I thought you might like this,' he says.

I take the little box from him, and he passes me and heads straight for the studio. I close the door and open the box. Inside is a silver chain with an 'H' on it. I follow him into the studio, not knowing how to react.

'I don't understand,' I say.

He looks flustered now and then embarrassed. 'It's a present,' he says, speaking to me as if I am a fool.

'I know that, but why?'

'Because I saw it and I thought of you. And, like I said, I thought you might like it. Do you want me naked?'

'Excuse me?'

'Do you want me naked today?'

'*Non,*' I say. 'Not today.'

The front door bangs shut and he turns his head in the direction of the sound.

'My father is here,' I explain.

'What? From Paris?'

'Yes.'

'Do you need me to go?' he asks.

'No,' I say. 'He is most probably gone for the rest of the day.'

'Okay.' He looks ill at ease now.

'Thank you, Adam,' I say, remembering the present in my hand. I take it out carefully, the chain is very fine. 'Really, thank you,' I say and smile.

He shrugs.

'Will you put it on for me?'

He takes the chain from me and I turn around. As I wait for him to fasten it I remember Ibiza, just before the first time Sid and I made love, when I had stood in front of him on the veranda of my apartment and he had wrapped his arms around me and carried me back indoors. If only I could have that time again. But there is no Sid now, only Adam. And a million feelings. I turn to face him. He does not move an inch and I am close enough to be in his arms, where I would fit perfectly. Just like I fitted Sid. And now I want his arms around me.

I look into his eyes, so like Sid's, but unlike Sid he is breathing. Living. His navy-blue eyes pull me in until I am lost. I am with my love again, one last time. Closing my eyes, I bring my hand to his chest and feel his heartbeat. He shudders as if I have just pierced his skin and touched the bare organ, but then he leans into my palm and takes a deep breath. I open my eyes and he is looking at me, his eyes intense and penetrating. We stay like this, as if mesmerised, while the air around us is alive with our charge, with the attraction that is drawing us together.

Eventually Adam kisses me, but this time his tongue pushes gently, tenderly, into my mouth. It makes me want to howl, but instead I wrap my arms around him. He stops kissing me.

'What about your father?' he whispers.

'Don't worry. He has left us,' I reply. 'But he would not be concerned. I am a grown woman doing what is natural.' I smile.

Still he does not move, so I pull him closer.

'I want you, Adam,' I say. I don't think I have ever wanted anyone more, not even Sid. I am suddenly aware of how risky life is, how fleeting the best moments, and how everything can be swept away in a split second. 'I want you,' I say again, and I can see waves of lust ripple through the navy blue of his eyes. I commit this to memory for the canvas. He grabs hold of me.

'I swear I have never wanted anyone more,' I whisper, and he pushes his lips against mine. We kiss for the longest time, squeezing our groins together, and I feel his erection inviting me to get closer. I open his trousers and take it in my hand. His breathing quickens and his hands find my body, touching me like he owns me.

Letting go of the flesh that I now want inside me, I lean up against the wall and he lifts me up and pulls me towards him so that his exposed erection touches my bare skin. My entire body begins to throb. It is like before, this feeling of Sid but without Sid. Adam slips into me easily as if he has done this a hundred times before. It feels familiar, as if we know each other's bodies already. I inhale him; so sweet, like Sid. It is Sid I taste and smell. I moan, which quickens his movement, and his breathing becomes heavier. My hips speed up, matching his rhythm, and the intensity between us builds until he comes inside me, which causes him to shout, just like Sid had in Ibiza. It takes me back there just before I come too. But soon, ecstasy gives way to devastation as huge waves of grief emerge and I begin to sob.

Adam catches my hair and pulls my head back so that I am looking up at him. The sudden pain shocks me into silence.

'Don't,' he says angrily.

Something flashes across his face. He draws back his arm and I shut my eyes, preparing myself for what is coming. But it doesn't happen. Instead, he lets go, pulls away from me and zips up his trousers, with no hint of the passion I had just witnessed. He leaves me before I can say anything and while his seminal fluid is still running down my legs, and then the knowledge of what I have just done hits me: it is the first time in my life that I have had unprotected sex. I had always been taught to be safe, and given Bebe's origins, which I have only recently discovered, her extreme drilling now makes more sense. However, it is not a warning of death nor illness that my body sends me right now, but its opposite. It whispers to me that there is a new life coming, pushing its way through the cracks. I lean back against the wall and slide all the way down and then swing round so that I am lying on my back with my legs raised against the cold surface of the wall. I place my hands on my belly. A premonition flashes in my mind and I see myself full of baby. I am becoming pregnant.

I lie there for a long time and let the emotions flood me. I swear I have never been so certain of anything in my whole life. I feel the sensation in my womb as it becomes aware that one of its eggs will finally make it. This part of my body is preparing itself for its first serious task: to continue the human life cycle. I remember back to that first day in the studio in Ibiza when I had pleaded with Sid to make me pregnant. That is what I wanted all along: to have a baby, something living to take me away from my constant longing for that which is dead.

I knew exactly what I was doing today, letting Adam come inside me. Yesterday with Raphael I would have let the same thing happen, but he had taken control, just as he always does, but especially that last time as he prepared to go to his girl in Milan. Life surges through me and I enjoy the sensation. And then I do what I always do at such times, I begin to paint, and the pictures come faster than any of the other ones before. As I create, my mind falls away. The energy possesses me and I let it, no longer afraid. The space beside me feels occupied and I turn to face it, just as I did yesterday.

'Sid,' I say as the air alters again, but today I keep my eyes open.

I watch but nothing comes, so I forget and I paint until I am totally spent and must stop to take food and rest. I fold myself into my bed and sleep – deep, dreamless sleep, nurturing and strengthening my body to help it grow this new life beginning inside me.

The front door bangs shut, pulling me out of my slumber and I immediately remember Papa. He is home again. All day he had stayed away, letting me know that he is still troubled by our exchange yesterday. He knocks lightly on my bedroom door.

'You are sleeping, *chérie*?'

'No, Papa. Please come in,' I reply, wanting to end our frostiness.

He comes in and sits on the edge of my bed as I sit up so that we are facing each other.

'I am so sorry, Papa,' I say and tears begin to well up.

He nods. 'It is the first time you have said these things to me. That you think so little of your papa upsets me.'

'But I don't. I was just angry, Papa. What you said hurt me.'

'So you wanted to hurt me too. But you told me the truth.'

'Yes,' I reply.

'I am sorry I made it so for you, Holly. But it is how I am and I will not change. Probably I cannot change now.' He bows his head and looks sad and old. It breaks my heart. I take his hand and kiss it.

'Papa, I do not want you to change. It is your life and I have no right to tell you how to live it. You love me. That is all that is important. And I love you.'

'Warts and all?' he adds.

'Yes,' I reply, 'warts and all.'

He kisses me on the forehead and wishes me sweet dreams and then leaves.

When I am alone my mind begins to race. For a long time my papa has told me of his wishes to be a grandfather and I picture his surprise when I tell him. Of course, he will wonder about the father, as will Bebe. And I will tell them that we three will raise this child together and it will never want for anything. This is how sure I am that I have seen the last of Adam. His reaction had been extreme. I had really believed that he was going to hit me. I run through the events in my head again. I suppose it was my huge tears that alarmed him, but his reaction –that was something else! And then he had just left. Right now as I lie and think of him, it is relief I feel, together with gratitude for my lucky escape, and I hope that I might never see him again.

SID II

Suzi, the girl whose heart I had broken, is with Carla, and they are sitting in what was once Dave and Carla's house but is now just Carla's. The people of my past. Shortly before I died, Dave had visited me in Ibiza and told me he was having an affair, much to my horror, making me a party to it – or at least that was how it had felt – and ending our thirteen-year friendship. And then my worst nightmare happened. I met Carla the last time I was in London and my silence told her everything she needed to know. That was where I left the story. Since then, she split up with Dave, but they got back together again after their baby was born. However, Carla had not been able to move past his infidelity, and now Dave is living with his secretary, Olga, and Carla is alone. And to think I had once believed they would be together forever!

This watching game is still frustrating, but at least now I have some control. Initially I had no handle on it at all and would hop from place to place at lightning speed, but now I can think about people without immediately being pulled towards them. The secret, I discovered, was awareness – I must simply know I am thinking, rather than allowing myself to get lost in my thoughts until they consume me.

I like coming here, especially these days, as this is easier to watch than watching my loved ones who are in danger. I watch Suzi make a fuss of baby Joaquín while Carla cooks in the kitchen, and then her boyfriend, Rob, joins her. He kisses her head and she smiles at him. My father had said that some day she would see that I had done the right thing when I left, but unfortunately, when she thinks of me, she still remembers all the years I did the wrong thing. She still resents me for staying with her when the truth was I didn't really love her. Who can blame her?

Carla is single and, although I have seen that Dave is not happy now, I can't help but think that she is better off without him, that they are better off apart. I join her in the kitchen and watch, seeing how motherhood has made her even more beautiful. She will not be alone for long.

Their lives go on. But mine is over.

I am a ghost in their living world, but even if I were still alive I would be dead to these people. The connection was broken in the last few months of my life. If I were living, I would be with my brother and that is where I go now.

My stomach hurls as I travel and I wonder if that feeling will ever go. Denzel is with Alice, stroking her belly and talking to his unborn child. He is blissfully unaware of the madness that is happening around him, lost in his second chance in life, the one thing he was sure would never happen in a million years. But it has, and now it is in danger of being taken away. He is tortured by a feeling of foreboding because he knows that if it collapses, he will not survive the heartbreak. I stay and watch for what feels like a short time. Time is a funny thing now; it moves differently to how it did when I was alive.

Then I travel to Adam Sheehan. He is alone in his hostel. I watch him and, not for the first time, I am struck by how like his father he is. This is what a young Denzel Anderson had looked like when he walked the planet aged fifteen. And yet no one can see what is so obvious. No one can see it, not even Holly; although this boy reminds her of me, she hasn't made the connection. I do not know what he will do, but his anger remains and I am worried for all of them. Now Holly is involved and it is inevitable where her relationship with Adam is heading. If I could do anything to stop this I would, and not just because I'm jealous. This boy is capable of doing great damage.

Thoughts of Holly take me to her as she paints furiously, moving around the studio like a dancer. I watch her now, just as I had done in Ibiza, and think her the most beautiful girl I have ever seen. What I would give to touch her now, to be with her and to make love to her again. I could return there, to those times in Ibiza, but I don't, nor do I go to the future where we get a shot at a life together. Both are too painful now, reminding me of what I have lost. I simply watch her in her present, longing for her.

Not a day passes where I don't go to be with her. For a long time she couldn't sense me. But then yesterday she did and I had felt almost alive again. But she had chosen to block me out. And I understand why. What good would it do her to see me? What good would it do her to know that my love for her has not left me in death? I know it doesn't help me. If anything it makes it worse.

I stand opposite her, crouching down and getting as close as I possibly can until I can feel her breath on my face. Even though I know it is pointless, I bring my lips to hers and kiss her, doing my best to remember how it had felt when I was alive. But today she stops and looks straight at me as if she can see me, and I feel alive again.

'Sid,' she says into the air.

It starts with a feeling of pressure, like the ceiling is pushing down on me, and then I am pulled away as if there is a magnet somewhere that holds a charge for me alone. For a minute I think I am moving on as I had seen Peggy do, but then I am set down in a place I don't recognise. I see a woman. She looks bewildered and confused, and tells me that she has only just arrived. She sees me and asks me where she is, and I get a feeling of déjà vu, taking me back to when I had first met Peggy.

Now I know exactly why I have been brought here. I put my arms around the woman, knowing that is what she needs most right now.

19

Adam's Eyes: Part III

I walk through the streets of London as if someone's in pursuit of me, knowing that I have to keep moving. If I stop, even for a minute, the thoughts flying through my mind will become unbearable. Everything is all messed up! I'd bought Holly the necklace. When I saw it in the charity shop I thought it was too much of a coincidence and knew I had to buy it. If I hadn't it would have plagued me – things like that do. So I bought it because I wanted to give her something after the other day. I told myself that it was to butter her up so that she'd be easier to manipulate, but there was more to it than that. I know that now, especially after what just happened.

I should never have had it off with her. Something happened in that room. I lost control. In spite of everything I like her. I seem to have developed some kind of attraction for her, and just thinking about it now makes me dislike her again. We had fucked bare, so God only knows what I might have floating around in my system now. How fucking stupid, Adam! You come to London to make your father pay for his sins, but instead you risk catching AIDS from a pretentious French bitch. You're a really smart young fella!

But I'd wanted her like nothing I've ever wanted before. That's the truth. It had felt incredible, and it allowed me to see that the times with Aoife were as insignificant as I'd suspected they were. Sex with Holly almost blew my head off. But then she'd started wailing like a banshee and alarm bells went off in my head. I didn't know what was happening and, as suddenly as the fear came, a rage gripped me so intensely that I almost hit her. Somehow I got myself out of there and took this seething anger with me. And here I am, walking with crazy thoughts going through my head, like what if Marie Sheehan had been mistaken all those years ago? What if she'd cried rape? What if she'd lied and here I was, avenging something that never happened? Marie had been a young girl and pregnant. Wouldn't it have been easier to lie, to say that Denzel Anderson had forced himself on her, rather than admit that she'd let him have her and that he'd rejected her? Wouldn't that have been easier and wasn't it possible? The more I think about it, the more it makes total sense to me.

As I walk the idea takes root in my head until I almost believe it, and the relief that comes is so comforting that it drives me to want to know, to have my story confirmed so that I can get on with my life and forget this mess that seems to be getting worse by the minute. I reach the hostel just as I make my decision. I'll call Marie right now while my desire to know is stronger than my fear. I've never asked her for anything in my life before and I'll remind her of that. She owes me this one thing. She owes me the truth.

Bernie answers immediately, as if she has been waiting for my call.

'Hello,' I say eventually.

'Jesus, Adam! It's really you! Are you okay, pet? Where are you? I've been so worried.' She starts to cry.

'Bernie, I'm sorry. I really didn't mean to put you through any of this.'

'So come home, Adam! Come home now.'

'I can't.'

'But you have to. Now!'

'I can't. Sorry. Listen, I need to talk to Marie.'

Silence.

'God, Adam, just come home. Your family needs you!'

'No, you don't, Bernie.'

She is sobbing hard and I get a strong feeling that something has happened.

'What's wrong. Tell me.'

She doesn't answer but continues to cry, and eventually her husband, Tommy, takes the phone from her.

'Adam, you need to come home,' he says.

'I can't do that, Tommy. I'm sorry.'

'Marie's dead.'

The words hit me as if they have physical substance. I can hear Bernie saying something now but I can't make it out.

'Adam, pet' – Bernie is on the line again – 'Please come home.'

'What happened?' I ask, but I already know the answer.

Silence.

'She killed herself, didn't she,' I say.

'Yes,' she whispers. 'You're all I have left, Adam.' Bernie starts to cry again and I remember how much I care about my sister, aunt – whatever the fuck she is.

'I *will* come home, but not just yet. I have something to do here first.'

'God, Adam, I'm scared. Where are you? Please don't do anything stupid! I can't lose you too!'

'I'll be fine and you'll be fine. Look, I'll call again soon.'

'You promise?'

'I promise.'

'I love you, Adam.'

That last bit takes me by surprise. 'I know, Bernie. I love you an' all.' I think it might be the first time I've ever said it to her.

I hang up the phone and start to feel really funny, as if I might throw up, so I go to the toilet in the hostel and, sure enough, I empty my stomach. It must be the shock. The Sheehan family has buried three people in less than a year. No wonder Bernie wants me home.

Marie is dead. She killed herself, and now it seems so obvious. We should all have seen it coming from a hundred miles away. She'd first tried when I was small – an overdose – and Mammy'd told us not to treat her any differently and she'd get over it. But she didn't. And every now and then, even after she'd met John, she'd go through 'dark times', as Mammy called them. Mammy was always there picking up the pieces, helping John to cope too. So this should be no surprise. My sister – my mother – hadn't a chance, really. And now she's dead. Although I think I should be feeling angry, instead, I feel really sad. And alone. And unable to reach out to anyone, just like when Mammy died. Anyway, there is no one to reach out to. Now there's just me and the question I need answered: was my mother raped, or did she lie? And there's only one person left who knows the answer. I grab my jacket and head for Rain Dogs.

I find the club almost empty and there's no sign of Denzel. I'm about to leave when I hear someone call out my name. I turn around and recognise Bill, the man my father referred to as his stepfather.

'It's Adam, isn't it?' he says and I nod. 'Bill,' he says and shakes my hand. 'Are you meeting Holly?'

'Not tonight. Is Denzel here?'

'It's his night off,' Bill explains. 'But maybe you'll join me for a drink.'

'Okay,' I say and let him buy me a drink. I get a warped sense of pleasure every time someone breaks the law on my account.

'Is beer okay?'

'Yes – thanks,' I reply.

He heads to the bar and I think about leaving. But the truth is, I don't want to be alone. Bill talks to the barman I'd met the last time I was here, but whose name I can't remember. I watch as they share a joke and then Bill joins me back at the table. He hands me a bottle of Becks and I thank him.

'You're Denzel's son,' he says after taking a long drink and catching me completely off guard. I could deny it, but what would be the point? I clear my throat.

'How did you know?'

'It's blatantly obvious. You're the living image of him. And I watched you with him the other night.'

'But he has no idea?'

Bill shakes his head.

'Denzel's too close to see it.'

'And Tim?'

'Your grandfather is a musical genius, but his inability to see what is right under his nose never ceases to astonish me. Does Holly know?'

I shake my head.

'I didn't think so. It's no coincidence that you've landed on our doorstep,' he says. This man likes to get straight to the point! 'Denzel and Alice are very dear to me,' he goes on. 'They're my family and I'm very protective of my family. I don't mean to be unpleasant but I am warning you that if you hurt them for whatever reason, I'll take it very personally.'

'Denzel raped my mother.'

Bill nods his head very slowly.

'You don't seem shocked by that?' I say, a bit put out that my revelation hasn't had the reaction I'd been expecting. He looks straight at me, and it dawns on me.

'You knew about my mother?' I say, unable to keep the shock out of my voice.

'Yes. Denzel told me. He feels tremendous guilt about what he did. He even thought about finding her but I told him not to. You see, he had just met Alice again and had a chance to start over again in life, something I know a little about. I didn't want him to do anything that might destroy that chance. Anyway, it happened a long time ago. What would have been the point?'

'Maybe me!' I say, unable to keep the emotion out of my voice.

'Well, of course, you weren't a consideration in any of it.'

He stops talking. I remain silent and finish my drink.

'I was hoping it wasn't true,' I say eventually. 'I was hoping that my mother lied.'

'But who knows what happened. These things are rarely clear cut. They were both so young.'

'But old enough to know the difference between right and wrong.'

'Right and wrong can be such relative terms.'

'I don't think so. It's one or the other and we make the choice,' I say. 'We make our own beds and then we have to lie in them.'

'Or maybe we are born to be the people we become.'

'I don't understand.'

'We all make mistakes and take wrong turns, but perhaps that's precisely what puts us where we need to be,' Bill says. 'None of us can rewrite history or change what we've already done, but we can let it alter what we do in the future. Maybe that's really where the choice lies.'

I shrug my shoulders, but I must admit, he makes a valid point.

'He's been through a lot, your father,' Bill adds. 'He's a good man, Adam. He deserves to be happy.'

'And my mother is dead,' I say.

'I'm very sorry to hear that.'

'Will you tell him about me?' I ask, changing the subject. I don't want his pity.

He shakes his head. 'He won't hear it from me. Are you going to stay in London?'

'I don't know,' I reply.

He looks at me for a long time until the barman comes over.

'You just can't keep away, mate!' the barman says, and I take the opportunity to say my goodbyes and escape.

20

The Best Place For The Past

It is Papa's last day in London. Today he travels back to Paris. I had thought about going with him, especially as I have not seen Adam since we had sex. A test yesterday confirmed what I had known without question almost immediately: I am pregnant. Already I feel the difference in my body. Yes, I could leave, but I must stay, if only to see what will happen next. My wish never to see Adam again has faded. Now I am curious to see whether he will come back, not because I want to be with him but because I want to understand what happened the last time we were together. There is more to this story than meets the eye, most certainly.

Papa and I have seen the city together, or at least all the major exhibitions, while he has been here, and much has been spoken about art. I love these times and hang on his every word. He sees so much, my papa, things that I miss. It humbles me. I could not bear it if we fell out, so I have told him I will love him warts and all, as he loves me. But I am glad that I told him the truth. He should know that I do not approve of his behaviour; perhaps he will be more discreet in future and save my feelings. There is a girl in Paris these days, a model that Raphael has photographed a lot, and she is spending time with Papa now. I saw it on the internet, these trashy sites I visit to find out about my papa. Imagine! What they see in him, these gold-digging girls, is clear to me, but what does he see in them, those young brainless creatures? That is the thing that disturbs me most. He has aged, matured, but his taste in women has stayed the same.

And what of my own attractions? I loved Sid and believed him a worthy man. He saw all of me, but what did I really know of a man I was with for so short a time. I have known Raphael most of my life and believe he wants only what he cannot have. He has been with many women who have tried to hook him with no success. They are too easy for him, I am the challenge. No, I do not think it is love. It is desire and a need to possess me. If I were to be with him, to marry him, I would cease to be a challenge and then what? There would always be another challenge, and my distrust would most certainly fuel his desire for others. In any case, I do not love him in that way. I could not pretend to play happy families. I have loved and know the value of it, but is that the truth? I tell myself I would have settled with Sid, but maybe it is easy to love completely when the one loved is dead.

Papa had told me I was making a mistake and that I should stay with Raphael. Now that I am pregnant perhaps that would be a good idea. I could marry him and we would raise this child together. And there is the possibility that this might be his baby. After all, I had sex with him shortly before Adam, and though we used a condom, contraception is never one hundred per cent safe. But no, I know what I know. It's Adam's. I am sure of it. Could I live with the lie and be with Raphael? The answer is no. That I can be thinking of doing that to him when he is trying to make it work with someone else is atrocious, and tells me he is better away from me.

'*Le talent, ça n'existe pas. Le talent, c'est d'avoir envie de faire quelque chose.* Who said that, and do you believe it?' Papa asks, pulling me from my internal world.

This is a game we have played since I was a child: a quote and I have to guess who.

'Ah, you are easy on me this time. It is one of my favourites, Jacques Brel. The quote translates as "The talent does not exist. The talent is to want to do something."'

'*Oui.* Very good,' says Papa. 'Do you believe it?'

'Yes, I think I do. The want produces the passion, which produces the art. *Non?*'

'Quite. You are a wonderfully flawed human being, *chérie,* just like your papa.' He is still hurting.

'I love you, Papa, and I know you have always loved me and I thank you for it.'

'You know that loving you is never a choice, *chérie.* From the moment you took your first breath I loved you. I was at the birth. I went as a sort of experiment to see how I would react and I was able to remain detached until you arrived. Then my detachment disappeared forever. To love you is all that is possible. It is my nature, just like painting.'

'Wow, Papa. You never told me that before.'

'Well, I think now is the time to tell you.'

I kiss him and we share a moment. We are fine again and my relief is immense.

'What next, *chérie?*' he asks, and my current situation comes back into my mind.

I think about blurting it out to him that I am having a baby and wonder what his reaction would be. But I say nothing because I have a feeling he would gather me up and take me away from here if he knew the truth.

'I will stay in London for a little longer,' I say.

'And you will move on from Sid?'

'Yes.'

'I do not like to see you like this, Holly. Life is waiting for you. Now. Today. You are missing this most important time as you dream about your Sid. You know that, don't you?'

'Yes, Papa.' I could argue with him, but there is no point because deep down I know there is no rational argument; what he says is true.

'And when you get back to Paris, you will never mention to Bebe that I let her secret out?'

'Of course not. Auntie Bebe! I never would have guessed!'

'Yes. Now forget about it.'

'Are there other things you need to tell me? Have I any brothers or sisters?'

'No, of course not. You must understand, Holly, I have always been honest with you, except for two times. And now you know them both.'

'Okay.'

'I think you could exhibit your work in Paris again soon. What you have done here is very good, *chérie*.'

'You think so?'

'Yes. I have watched you grow as an artist in front of my eyes and now you are fully formed and ready to explore. It is funny because I did not mature as an artist until much later, but then I suppose I had a late start, unlike you. You know, you were painting as a little tot. I still remember you huddled down beside me, watching me and copying me. You were so cute, mini Holly.'

'I remember,' I say and smile. My childhood with my papa had been precious. Sid had not had the same good start, and now I had met Tim Harris, one of the two people who had made Sid's early years so hard. Yes, I have been blessed. I kiss my father again.

'What was that for?' he asks.

'For nothing and everything!'

He smiles and catches hold of my hand.

'Are you finished in New York, Papa?'

'For now. But I will go back in a few months. The show in the New Year will be huge, they tell me.'

'I am excited for you.'

'And perhaps you can be included?'

'*Non*. My time will come, like you always say. Although it would be very tempting to have my work hang in the Guggenheim, I do not want to piggyback on the work of my papa.'

'*Chérie*, I am proud of you. You are your father's daughter. Now I must go, so kiss your Papa.'

I kiss and hug him.

'You will keep in touch, of course,' he says.

'Yes, Papa.'

'You know, you seem different somehow these past few days. Is there something you need to tell me?'

I flush red but say nothing, not wanting to lie.

'Mmmm, it must be a boy,' he says. '*Chérie*, do not fall so soon and so quickly. *Non*. Consider what I have said to you, even a little bit. Keep your love for your family, and flirt with what comes from outside.'

I nod and wonder again how he will take my news. Our little family is soon to grow.

Papa leaves me with just enough time to get ready to see Denzel. He had called earlier and invited himself to the apartment.

When Denzel arrives his reaction reminds me of his visit to Paris earlier in the year when he had seen our French home.

'This place is amazing!' he says.

'Yes, my papa knows his properties. So you want some coffee?' I ask.

'Ja, that would be lekker,' he says.

'That means yes?'

'It does, ja!' He smiles.

'Thanks for coming,' I say.

'Ah thought it was time to see your humble abode, although there isn't anything humble about it.'

I laugh. 'Jean-Claude is not a humble man.'

'Jean-Claude is your papa bear?'

'My "papa bear"! I like that very much. Yes, you just missed him. He left to go back to Paris today.'

'Ah missed him in Paris too. Ah guess we are just not destined to meet.'

'It seems so.'

'Ja, Paris. It feels like a long time ago.'

'Even though it wasn't. Yet so much has changed since then. You are soon to have a baby.'

I get an urge to blurt it out 'And now me too,' but I don't. I get the coffee and we sit by the window.

'This is an amazing view,' he says.

'Yes. My father likes to keep an eye on a city's dowry,' he says.

'Ah like that,' he replies, nodding.

We sit in silence and drink.

'It was lovely to meet Tim,' I say eventually.

'Ja. He is a good man. Ah get the feeling he is very different to how he was before.'

'Before Sid died?'

'Ja.'

'Do you still talk to him? Sid I mean.'

'Not so much now. Ah guess Ah don't want to freak Alice out any more than Ah do already.'

He smiles and I remember his smile. It is quite something. I only really noticed it after Ibiza; maybe he didn't smile so much in those days.

'She's great,' he continues. 'Ah still can't believe she's back in ma life after all this time.'

'You are happy, Denzel?'

'Very happy. Ah could never have imagined being this happy.'

'But yet you look scared,' I say.

'Well, it could easily come tumbling down. Couldn't it?'

I know that feeling. A few years ago I would have told him to enjoy it now and allow for the possibility that it just might work out. But that had been before Sid, where it had all gone horribly wrong, despite my good feelings.

'So how is Adam?' Denzel asks.

'I don't know,' I reply. 'I haven't seen him for a while.' I do not want to go into it.

'We all really liked him. Ah told him he could come play in the club some night and Ah meant it. But he never got back to me. Can you remind him when you see him?'

'Yes,' I say. *If I see him.*

'And Alice said you should both come for dinner soon. Maybe you can come this week and we can discuss when he will play in the club. Ja?'

'Yes, that would be nice,' I say.

Denzel looks into the distance and again I see an expression cross his face, one that I had seen in Ibiza many times and in Paris. His life has moved on but he is still haunted. It reminds me of Pia.

'I've been thinking about Pia recently,' I say.

Denzel looks at me. 'If she's still hanging out with Marco, tread carefully.'

'Yes. He is the worst of news.'

'Sometimes the past is best left in the past,' he says and his face darkens.

'Is there something you want to tell me, Denzel?' I ask. He looks at me in a way that encourages me to continue. 'When I saw you in Paris, there was something you wanted to tell me but you didn't. Is it that same thing?'

He nods. 'Ah remembered some stuff there and Ah wish Ah hadn't. Ah never told Alice and Ah tell her everything, but this one thing Ah couldn't bring maself to tell her. Just before we got back together something happened to her, and it has convinced me that Ah can never tell her ma story because Ah think Ah'll lose her for good. That would kill me.'

'Can you lay it to rest, this awful thing? Sid said he felt so much better after he spoke to his father – your father – and set things right between them. Can you do the same with this situation?'

'Ah don't think so, Holly. Ah wouldn't know how to go about it.'

'Then can you forget, Denzel? Leave the past in the past, just like you said?'

'What if Ah can't?'

'Then maybe you have to do something.'

'Do you believe in karma?' he asks.

'*Absolument!*'

'You are sure?'

'Of course! Every action has a consequence. That is logical. That is life.'

'Well, Ah did something and ran away from it so it had no consequences for me.'

'But that is where you are wrong, Denzel. Of course it had a consequence. You running away from it didn't stop it. It continues in you. So perhaps the thing to do is to stop running. Then a new consequence will result. You cannot change it but can you rectify it perhaps.'

'Ah don't think so.'

'Well, perhaps life has already rectified it and part of that process involved you running away. Can you accept that?'

'Maybe.'

'And you torturing yourself will have consequences until you stop. You have to let go of your past.'

'But how do Ah let go?'

'That is the big question. How indeed! You want to tell me?' I say.

He smiles.

'Alice is the most important thing now and your baby that is coming.'

He nods.

'And you think if you tell her you will lose her, them both?'

'Ja! For sure.'

'So you have two options. Don't tell her and live with the consequences. Or tell her and live with the consequences.'

'And what if the consequences of both sets of actions are the same?'

'Well, why are we having this pointless conversation then?'

He begins to laugh.

'Sid told me he loved how you laughed,' I say.

'Really?'

'Yes. He said it made him laugh, that it was infectious. He was right.'

'Ah still can't bring maself to read his diary.'

'I understand. It contains his personal thoughts. There may be things in there he didn't tell for a reason. They were his thoughts alone.'

'You wouldn't read it, would you?'

'No,' I reply. 'I keep my memories in here.' I put my hand on my chest.

He smiles.

'And there are things you do not tell your Alice that perhaps she does not want to know.'

'Do you believe time heals like they say?'

'Only time will tell,' I say and we both laugh more than the joke deserves. But it feels good.

21

Intimate Exposures

I can hear the sound of his guitar in the distance, which lets me know he is where I had expected to find him. I wonder if he has placed himself there knowing I would come, for he could so easily have got lost in the huge London crowd. I gather myself together before I turn the corner. I have always loved that phrase, even though I am not entirely sure what it means. Where was I that I required to be gathered up? Had my body parts strayed away from me, running in different directions just like my mind? And what of the spirit? Does that ever need to be gathered up? Can it fly in more than one direction? My mind travels, as do my feet, despite my wish to be one whole, centred human being.

When he sees me he stops playing in the middle of his tune and starts to pack up.

'I will get us some coffee,' I say and he nods.

My coffee tastes funny. It is beginning, this baby inside me, telling me what it does not want. I wonder if it knows that I am about to sit with its father.

Adam joins me and immediately takes a drink of his coffee. His hands are shaking.

'Adam, I do not understand what happened the last time I saw you,' I say.

He takes another drink of coffee. 'We had sex,' he says sarcastically, but his face reddens.

'It was your first time?' I ask.

'Was it yours?' he replies and it makes me smile. 'Why did you cry?'

'I was emotional, that is all.'

'It wasn't anything I did?'

'No, not at all. I really enjoyed it.'

'Me too,' he says.

I put my hand on his, expecting him to pull away, but he doesn't.

'Can we go back to yours and do it again?' he asks.

'Yes,' I reply, glad of the chance to appease my increased sex drive and, conveniently forgetting our last farewell, telling myself that I had misjudged the situation, even though deep down I know I hadn't. He had come close to harming me.

We leave our coffee and walk hand in hand back to the apartment. Once we are inside I take his guitar case from him and lead him into my bedroom. I have seen him naked, masturbated in his presence and had sex with him, yet this is the first time he has seen my bedroom. He wraps his arms around me and I think of Sid as I lean into the space that seems to fit me perfectly. I lift my head and Adam begins to kiss me. The feel of his beard reminds me that I am here in the present with him, that Sid is gone, and as we kiss I remember what my papa had said: 'Let go of your past, *chérie*.' But I ask the same thing Denzel asked: how do I let go?

My body takes over as I give into what is happening below, regardless of where my mind is. I feel Adam's erection and I begin to remove my clothes. He does the same until we are both naked and standing in front of each other. He touches my face, my neck, my breasts, my stomach. And then he reaches between my legs. I place my hand on his and guide him. I show him what to do and I climax quickly.

'You are a fast learner,' I whisper to him and he smiles. Now I wish there was no beard, that his face was smooth like Sid's.

'Would you ever shave this off?' I ask and he shrugs.

I lie on the bed and he lies on top of me.

'Do you have johnnies?' he asks.

'Sorry, I don't know what you mean,' I say.

'Condoms,' he explains.

Oh dear, Adam, it is far too late for that now!

'It is okay,' I say and momentarily think about telling him that I am pregnant. His navy-blue eyes look at me waiting for an explanation, and however I frame the words in my head they will not come. 'I am on the pill,' I say. 'And I don't sleep around like this.'

He looks at me, trying to decide whether to believe me or not, and I wonder if the lie shows upon my face. I conclude that it doesn't as he pushes himself inside me. It feels incredible, like my hormones are supercharged, but also I feel exposed and the reward for this is intense pleasure. His bare flesh, now wet and throbbing, massages the most intimate part of me. My sensitivity is heightened, and I swear I can feel his very essence seeping into my flesh and my bones where I will carry it forever. I climax, it happens again and again until I lose count. We make love until we are both exhausted and fall asleep in each other's arms. When I wake up Adam is still beside me sleeping peacefully. The room smells of sex and something else. Him? Us? Or maybe it is the new life inside me, the one I am keeping secret. I take a deep breath and almost feel drunk.

Adam stirs and opens his eyes.

'You're not sleeping,' he says.

'No, not now,' I reply.

'Are you okay?' he asks.

'I think so. Are you?'

'I guess so.'

'We are a certain pair,' I say and smile.

'Do you think we are a pair?' he asks.

'It is just a phrase, Adam!' I reply my defences taking over. Now that he is opening up to me, something in me is closing down.

He turns away from me and goes back to sleep.

I sleep deeply. These days I am sleeping for such a long time and I wonder what tiring feat is in front of me that my body feels it necessary to get so much rest. Everything is changing, at least physically. Mentally, I am the same old mess.

A phone ringing somewhere to my left brings me back to the waking world. I open one eye and see that Denzel is trying to reach me so I answer.

'Hi, Holly, it's Alice.'

It is not who I expected! 'Hello! Is everything okay?' I ask.

'Yes. I just wanted to invite you and Adam over for dinner. I'm sorry, you sound like you've been sleeping.'

'Yes.'

'Sorry!'

'When would you like us to come?'

'Tonight.'

I look at the clock and see that it is 10 a.m., earlier than I normally rise. Then Adam stirs beside me.

'Just one minute, please,' I say, sounding very official even to my own ears.

'Will you come to Denzel's for dinner tonight?' I ask him. He looks shabby and sleepy.

'Okay,' he replies.

'Yes. What time, please?' I say into the phone.

'About seven thirty? Is that okay?'

'Yes. We will be there.'

'Right, see you both then.'

'Yes.'

'Goodbye.'

'Goodbye.'

I set the phone down and wonder how I should behave in this unfamiliar situation. But when Adam begins to kiss my neck, all my uncertainty disappears and I simply do what feels natural.

22

Dinner With The Andersons

We get to Denzel's place at seven thirty on the dot and I realise that our punctuality is down to my companion. Adam is the timekeeper and I am on time for something for the first time in maybe my life. It makes me think me of Sid, and I dwell on the fact that we never had such demands placed on us as a couple. How is it possible that this man I loved so much was with me for such a short time and yet now his memory seems to suck the joy from almost everything? It is not such a healthy thing, so perhaps Papa is right: it is not love at all. But is it possible to deny it, to simply switch it off? I don't think so or I would have done it by now.

Alice answers the door and I am greeted by a different woman to the one I met that first night. I suppose now that I am safe in the arms of someone else there is less for her to fear from me. Perhaps we might even become friends of a sort. How funny female behaviour is, so susceptible to the massive insecurities that society continually fuels with its constant pressures. The world likes nothing better than to set us against each other in our quest to win over the opposite sex and, more often than not, we dance along to its tune.

Adam and I sit at the table, and Denzel joins us with a bottle of champagne while Alice prepares dinner in the kitchen.

'It's just us four tonight,' Denzel says as he pours. I decide that I will risk one glass of champagne as refusing would only draw attention and require explanation.

'Cosy,' I reply. It is a word that I have discovered only recently and come to love.

'For sure,' Denzel replies.

Once he has filled our glasses, he disappears into the kitchen. Adam and I sit in silence. I do not look at him yet I feel his eyes upon me, and I know that if I were to look in his direction he would look away. Still he shuts me out and so I play his stupid game. Denzel rejoins us with Alice by his side.

'Denzel, you grabbed me during a very vital part of the cooking process!' she says, looking flustered.

'Ah'll be quick, Alice. Here's to a good night,' he says and raises his glass to toast the occasion.

I am touched by his sentimentality. I take a little sip and am shocked to find that it is ill-received: baby bear does not like champagne. The moment passes as Alice disappears back into the kitchen. Adam follows her and I wonder what he is doing. Denzel watches too, probably wondering the same thing, but he says nothing. The boy is not predictable and does things without any consideration for other people. It must be liberating to be like that – self-serving. I believed I was until I stumbled upon this master of the craft.

'How is everything?' Denzel asks me, gesturing towards Adam.

'Okay, I suppose,' I say.

'He seems like a decent boy.'

'Decent? How do you mean?'

'A good human being.'

I say nothing but my facial expression makes Denzel smile.

'It's never easy between men and women,' he says. 'Did you speak to him about playing at the club?'

'No, I thought it would be better coming from you.'

'Fair enough. You've heard him? He's good, ja?'

'Yes. He is very good.'

'You sound more sure about his artistic gifts than about his merits as a person.'

'I seem to see those more easily in other people than in him. Are you okay – after our chat the other day?'

'Ja. It gave me a lot to think about.'

Adam comes in carrying some food.

'She's put you to work, Adam. That's why Ah stay away from the kitchen if Ah can.' Denzel winks and flashes his gap-toothed smile.

'No, Denzel, I keep you away from the kitchen because you are a liability,' Alice says as she joins us.

'Ja, she works alone but Ah fetch and carry for her.'

'Just like Adam is doing for me now,' Alice adds with an air of suggestion – but perhaps I am just being paranoid.

'The food looks amazing,' I say, wanting to flatter Alice, to win her over, for Denzel's sake more than my own. But there is also a part of me that wants her to like me as Adam seems to like her.

'Thank you,' she replies.

'Ja, Alice is one of the best cooks Ah've ever come across. The food tastes great but she also manages to make it look great too. Ja, she's an artist in the kitchen.'

A smile passes between the couple and I look at Adam. He is watching them too and I am hungry for his attention.

We all sit down at the table and help ourselves to the food. This is a spectacular spread, just as it was the first time I was here.

'Is dinner like this every night?' I ask.

'Yep, except for the nights Ah cook,' Denzel says. 'Which are not so many for that very reason.'

'Yes, I'm the chef in the family,' says Alice.

'And Ah'm the gofer.'

'So Adam has been telling me about his music,' Alice says and I immediately become interested. She waits for him to speak but he remains silent, so she fills us in instead. 'He's been playing guitar since he was a small boy and he's come here to see if he can make a career. And he writes his own stuff.'

'That is something Ah wanted to talk to you about actually,' Denzel says. 'How about a slot at Rain Dogs?'

'That would be great,' Adam says. 'Thank you.'

I cannot help but notice a change in Adam. He is almost humble and I wonder if that has anything to do with the new development between us. We are still far from close but our love-making must have altered something.

'Denzel, you should take Adam to see Depeche Mode!' Alice bursts in.

'Ja,' Denzel says, 'why not? Clive was meant to come but can't, and ma missus won't join me.'

'I can't think of anything worse with this belly,' Alice says pointing to her stomach. I take a look at what is ahead for me.

'It's not long now, honey bunny,' Denzel says and smiles. 'You want to come, Adam?'

'When is it?' Adam asks.

'Tomorrow night.'

'Okay,' he says eventually.

'Great! So it's decided,' says Alice. 'So, how did you two meet?'

I give Adam a chance to speak and when he doesn't, all eyes fall on me.

'I saw him in a coffee shop near where I live and the first thing I noticed about him was his hands.'

'How strange!' Alice says. ' His hands?'

'Well, I had decided that I would study hands while I was in London as a theme for my work and Adam's hands turned up in my line of vision.' I do not look at Adam but I can guess exactly how he is looking at me now.

'Denzel tells me you painted a picture of him in Ibiza,' Alice says.

'Yes,' I reply. 'But it was a Denzel of a long time ago – not recognisable as the person I know today.'

I remember our times in Ibiza and a look passes between Denzel and me.

'I heard about the state he was in back then,' Alice says laying her hand upon his arm territorially. 'An old school friend of ours found him in Ibiza.'

'Ja, Ah was at the beck and call of cocaine back then. But that was before Ah found you again, Alice. For sure. You've been the making of me, but then you always brought out the best in me.'

Alice smiles. 'Well that goes both ways, Denzel,' she replies and I notice how much she is softened by his words.

I watch them and can see the connection between them. I wonder if there is such a link developing between me and Adam. I look Adam's way but he is watching the other couple intensely, as if by scrutinising them something of great importance might be revealed to him. It makes me wonder whether my questions about relationships, about love, are his questions too. Despite all his bravado maybe he is looking for a similar kind of relationship as I am.

Adam asks if he can use the bathroom. His request reminds me of a child asking permission to leave the table.

'He seems like a lovely boy,' Alice says when he is out of earshot. I do not like how she emphasises the word 'boy'. Although she smiles, it is not real. She is pretending, trying to like me but she doesn't.

'Yes. He is very lovely,' I agree.

'What is his own music like, Holly?' she asks, making it feel like a loaded question.

'Wonderful!' I say, lying rather than give her the pleasure of knowing I have not yet heard it. 'It will be good for him to play in the club. How is the club going, Denzel?' I ask, wanting to move the conversation away from this woman's questions.

'Very well! Ja, Bill is amazing for networking. He knows so many people and makes the right business connections without even having to try. The number of big acts he's managed to get on our books for the next six months is phenomenal. Clive and I can't believe the people he convinces to play in our small unknown venue. And Ah've managed to get some of the biggest DJs signed up thanks to Titus. You remember Titus?'

'Of course,' I reply. 'Who could forget Titus!' It brings Pia to mind and again I think about contacting her.

'Ja, Alice met Titus and he made an equally big impression on her!'

Alice nods. 'You only meet someone like Titus once.'

'So you still have a connection to Titus, Denzel?' I ask.

'Ja. Just before I left Ibiza he sat me down and told me that Ah was like a son to him. It just about knocked me off ma feet, that. So ja, we are still in contact.'

'And do you feel a similar bond to him?' I ask.

'Ja, Ah suppose Ah do. It was weird when Tim came back in ma life after having pretty much disowned me the first time. But Titus always accepted me. He's looked out for me from day one.'

'When you met him in Ibiza, you mean,' I say.

'Ja.'

'Has Tim met Titus?' I ask.

'Who's Titus?' Adam asks as he rejoins us.

'He's a friend of mine from Ibiza where Ah met Holly. Has she told you anything about Ibiza, Adam?'

'No,' he replies.

'I am thinking of contacting Pia again,' I say, wanting to take us away from the subject of Ibiza.

'Ja, where is she now?'

'I believe she is back in Madrid. I've been thinking about her a lot and it makes me think I should contact her.'

'Is she clean?' Denzel asks.

'I have no idea.'

'When do you think you would like me to play at the club?' Adam butts in.

'We're starting an acoustic night on Thursdays so how about you come and do the next one? How long could you play for?' Denzel asks.

'All night if you want me to,' Adam says.

'Well, how about you do two one-hour sets and we see how that goes?' he says.

'Great!' Adam responds. 'And thanks – really.'

'Ja, it's not the easiest setting up in a new city. Ah was lucky, thanks to ma father.'

'Are all your family in Ireland?' Alice asks.

'Yes,' Adam replies.

'Your parents and your siblings?'

'I was raised by my grandmother. My mother came to London when she was a young girl and got pregnant.'

'That sounds a lot like ma story,' Denzel says. 'Ma mother got pregnant here in London too and went back to South Africa to have me.'

'My mother never really liked me very much,' Adam says.

I sit back and watch as Adam reveals himself, allowing a few layers to peel away.

'I know that feeling,' Alice chimes in. 'My mother and I have never got on. Are you still in touch?'

'No, she killed herself.'

His words land in the room, heavy and conspicuous.

'I am so sorry, Adam,' Alice says.

I begin to feel nauseous – it comes upon me all of a sudden and makes me wonder if the alcohol was such a good idea – and I am forced to excuse myself from the table. I get to the toilet just in time, and after I have emptied the contents of my stomach, my head spins a little and my legs feel weak so I rest on the floor.

As I sit there I think about Adam. How bizarre that his mother killed herself, just like Sid's. Although my rational mind knows that many people kill themselves, I can't help thinking that this is significant, another link to Sid. But of course I link everything to Sid in some way or other these days. Eventually I pull myself together and when I get back to the table I find the conversation flowing. The topic is music and Denzel is talking about his father. I sit in silence, listening and enjoying this talkative version of Adam and feeling sorry that we do not seem to have this natural flowing conversation when it is just the two of us.

'Are you okay?' Denzel asks.

'Sorry, I think I might have to leave now,' I reply. 'I don't feel so great.'

'I hope it wasn't anything you ate,' Alice says edgily.

'Not at all. The food was great. But I have been feeling a little ill recently.'

Adam and I quickly say our goodbyes and leave. Adam looks like he is annoyed that we have to go but he still comes with me.

He walks me home in silence and I don't say anything either, thankful for the space. London is still alive but it is starting to quieten down. I like it most of all when it is like this. I enjoy the speed of the people as they pass us by; it gives me just enough time to commit a piece of them to memory. At the front door of the apartment I ask Adam if he will stay but he says no, not tonight. I am relieved as my earlier sickness is still lingering. He leaves me without saying when we will next meet. He just assumes that we will. It is nothing unusual.

Just as I am preparing for bed my phone rings. I answer it, expecting it to be Denzel but I am surprised to find it is Alice again.

'Are you okay, Holly?' she wants to know.

'Yes,' I reply, taken aback by her concern. If I need someone to turn to with my problems, it will not be this woman.

'I just wanted to call because you didn't seem yourself tonight.'

And what does she know about what it is to be myself, I wonder.

'You don't like me very much, Holly,' she says eventually.

'*Non*,' I reply.

'Because I wasn't very nice to you when you first came here. I'm sorry. I guess I was a little afraid of your relationship with Denzel.'

This pushes me from my high horse a little.

'I am shocked to hear you say this,' I say.

'Me too,' she says, and the line goes quiet until she asks if I'm still there.

'*Oui*,' I reply.

She waits a little while, and although I am almost certain I know what it is she is waiting for, I debate whether to give it to her.

'Well, I've said what I wanted to say, so goodbye,' she says eventually.

'Alice?' I say, just before she hangs up.

'Yes.'

'You have nothing to worry about. I am not a threat.'

'Thank you,' she says and ends the call.

23

The Friend In Need

I wake up alone and it feels odd for a while. How soon a person can get used to things like an extra body in bed! Once I am fully awake I feel nauseous, my body reminding me that it is pregnant. My bump, which is in my imagination only, as my belly has not altered, brings me comfort and I visualise myself in the future when I am big like Alice. It will be odd, but nice too. Still, I walk on tenter hooks with Adam as I travel through these new hormone-infused emotional times. There have been a few occasions when I thought I might tell him about the baby but something always stops me. I suppose I know it would be the wrong thing. This is my baby, the something new that I have craved for so long. My child belongs in my future. However, it does not feel as if Adam does. Again, last night, we left things hanging, and if I want to see him he will play tomorrow night at Rain Dogs. I will go, of course.

Eventually I feel better and take myself to the studio to paint. I forget about the mind stuff – the demand for explanations – and simply get lost in allowing the images to fall on to the canvas. I love this feeling – pure trust in an energy I do not understand and have no wish to, for it would break the magic. I move around and allow the movements of my body to travel down my arm into my hand, to express themselves on the canvas. Free and flowing, everything feels in sync now and everything other than what I am doing disappears. Now there is only what is being born through me, not of me, born from somewhere else, from another realm I can feel with great intensity but cannot see or touch. If I tried to touch it it would slip through my fingers like running water. I paint until my body tells me to stop for sustenance, fuel.

Once my hunger has been silenced by my usual ration of croissants and cheese, which the little one has no apparent objection to, I am all set to take a nap when my phone rings. A number I do not know flashes on the screen and curiosity makes me to answer. I recognise her voice immediately and it shocks me back to reality.

'Pia? Are you okay?'

'No, Holly. I'm in a lot of trouble,' she tells me, her voice sharp like a siren.

'What has happened?' I ask.

'It's Marco.'

Well, of course it is Marco, I am tempted to say but don't. 'What has he done?' I say instead.

She begins to cry.

'Where are you?' I ask.

'I'm in London. I called Paris and Bebe told me you were here too.'

'What are you doing in London?' I ask, still not sure whether to open up my door to her. I know how bad her habit is and our friendship is distant now.

'Marco brought me here a few days ago.'

'You sound high,' I tell her, setting her habit between us again, just as I had done back in Ibiza.

The line goes silent.

'I told you I can't be around that any more,' I say.

'I know Holly, but I need your help. Please If there was anyone else I wouldn't be calling you. I swear!'

I stay silent.

'There's no one else I can turn to! I have nowhere else to go! Please! Holly!'

I wait while my friend pulls on my heartstrings. Deep down I know that I am bringing a lot of trouble on myself. Marco is definitely someone to be avoided, but this is my friend from art school. I can remember how she was before Marco, and although the friendship has been redundant for a time, it is not gone completely. I feel it now like a real physical part of me.

'Do you remember how to get here?' I ask.

'Yes,' she says and I am reassured by the relief I hear creep into her voice. She is desperate.

'Come now,' I tell her.

'Thank you so much, Holly. You won't regret it,' she says.

'I hope not Pia, for both our sakes,' I reply.

Less than an hour later she is at my front door, looking as if she has been in a bad accident.

'*Mon Dieu*, Pia! Your face! Come in and tell me what happened.'

She comes into my home at a junkie's pace and, once I have armed her with the strongest coffee I can make, she begins to tell me her story. She speaks in French and I fall back into my native tongue quickly.

Marco had bribed her into coming to London in the usual way – drugs, always the promise of drugs and she will do anything. But this time he had a special plan for her over here. He sent her to do a drug deal and it had all gone horribly wrong. The three men had roughed her up and then refused to pay. She had called Bebe who had told her I was here. What were the chances of me being here? Surely it was a sign that redemption was possible? So she decided she would leave Marco once and for all and come here to me.

I try to get her to go to a hospital but she refuses. Marco will find her there, she says, and she is scared of what he will do to her because she didn't get the money. She assures me that Marco does not know about my apartment and so there is little chance of him finding us, but something still makes me anxious. Perhaps it is a fear for the new life inside of me, and with it, an extra level of caution about such things.

'Pia, I think we should call Denzel,' I say and she agrees.

I make the call and am not disappointed. He will help us. A short time later the door bell rings and Pia looks panicked in a way that makes me glad I had called Denzel.

I open the door to Denzel. 'Prepare yourself for a shock,' I say and lead him through to the front room.

'Jesus, Pia! What the fuck happened to you?' he says.

She begins to cry.

'Fucking Marco! Tell me what happened from the start.'

She tells Denzel and he listens carefully. Once she has finished, he tells her not to worry, that he knows exactly who can sort this out.

'Ah'll let Titus know what's happened,' he says and takes his phone out.

'No, Denzel! Marco will kill me!' she says.

'Na, he'll kill Marco is what he'll do. This is his fault.'

'Come on, Pia,' I say. 'Let's get you cleaned up.'

I run a bath for her and give her some fresh towels.

'Thank you, Holly. I appreciate this.'

'It's okay. I'm just sorry this has happened to you.'

She begins to cry again.

'I want to get clean, Holly. Really I do.' She hands me her bag. 'Take this and get rid of my stuff. I'm done.'

'It will be fine,' I say before I leave her alone. 'Denzel and Titus will sort it all out.'

Back in the front room Denzel is still speaking on the phone. He is talking in Afrikaans so I assume it is Titus on the other end. I wait until he finishes.

'Fucking Marco! What was he thinking? Ah could fucking kill him, Holly. Seriously. Ah'd forgotten what a fucking moron he is. Titus said he doesn't deal with Marco any more but he knows who he's working with now. And he'll sort him out.'

'What does that mean, Denzel?' I ask.

'He's a dead man, Holly. Pure and simple.'

'*Mon Dieu*! You are serious!' I always knew that Marco and Denzel were involved with some bad people, but to hear that someone was going to be killed, even if that someone was an ape like Marco, makes my blood run cold.

'Ja, for sure. Pia doesn't need to worry any more, although Ah think you might want to put her on a plane back to her folks. She's a mess, ja, and probably a bit much for you to handle.'

'I think she wants to stay here,' I say.

'Na! Holly do you really want to go through all that? She should get into rehab. This is a bit much for you. Na?'

Perhaps if this were another time I would disagree, but now that I am pregnant my priorities have to change.

'Yes, you are right,' I say. 'I will tell her to go back to Madrid and get cleaned up. She asked me to get rid of her stuff .' I hold up her bag.

Denzel raises an eyebrow. 'And you're sure she has nothing with her in the bathroom?'

I open her bag and find it empty except for some make-up and an empty wallet.

'There is nothing in here!' I say.

'Ja, they probably cleaned her out and took all her gear as well. Or maybe she has it with her in the bathroom. You can't take her at her word. You know the drill here, ja! She's a junkie!'

I nod. Of course, Denzel is right.

'And Marco probably has her passport. Ah know that fucker. Titus said he will make sure it is put in your postbox tonight.'

'I had no idea Titus was so powerful,' I say.

'Ja, he is a good man to know in circumstances like these, although you could argue that it's only because of him that circumstances like these arise in the first place.' Denzel smiles and makes me smile too.

'So you girls will be okay. Ja? Marco doesn't know where you live, right?'

'*Oui.* I mean no, he has never been here, and Pia said she has never told him about this apartment.'

'Are you sure?' he asks. 'Don't take any chances. Titus will work fast but there could be enough time for Marco to pay you a visit if he knows where you live. Look Ah'll stay here just in case. Titus said he'd call when it's done.'

'Thank you, Denzel!'

'Like Ah said Ah promised ma little brother that Ah'd look after you and Ah will. Part of this is ma fault. Ah should have insisted that Marco was sorted properly last time but Ah didn't. And Titus gave him a last chance too and he just messed it up. The world will be a better place without that asshole.'

I have to agree, but it still feels surreal. And wrong.

'He will really be killed?' I ask again.

'Ja, and let's just hope it happens quickly and things don't get any more messed up.'

He speaks about death so matter-of-factly, like we are arranging something quite ordinary. It makes me crave normality.

'Shall I make us some more coffee?' I ask.

'Ja, coffee would be good. Ah'll call Alice and tell her not to expect me until she sees me. And Holly?'

'Yes,' I say, interrupting my journey to the coffee pot and turning around to face him.

'Be careful what you wish for,' he says.

'How do you mean?'

'Ah got a bad feeling the other night when you were talking about reconnecting with Pia and here we are.'

'Yes,' I say, 'I should have left the past in the past!'

'Ja, for sure.'

24

Adam's Eyes: Part IV

I give the guy the money and he hands over the white powder. It takes me all the way back to the playground in Dublin. But today I am buying rather than selling. It's a present for my father. A lot has happened in the last few days, and I feel like I'm on a rollercoaster with no idea when or where the ride will stop. In my mind I travel back through the events that have led me here to this dodgy Camden backstreet.

News of Marie's suicide was a shock and sent me on the road to my father to tell him everything, but it was Bill I had seen. Bill knows who I am. He had seen the family resemblance, said it was obvious, and yet to everyone else it seems to go unnoticed. Our conversation revealed that he knew about my mother, that my father had told him about the rape and had actually thought about looking for the girl he'd raped, but Bill had advised him to forget. Bill told me that my father regretted what he'd done and had set about convincing me to let it be, not to rock the apple cart, as Mammy would have said. Denzel was happy and deserved to be happy, Bill said. He assured me that my secret was safe with him and I believed him, trusted him, but then my judgement has shown itself to be flawed recently. The reality is, I can trust no one.

The next day I went to the coffee shop to busk, hoping I would bump into Holly, thinking that sex would be a distraction from how bad I was feeling. And she had come and taken me back to her flat where she'd given me what I wanted – that and so much more! As we'd stood naked in front of each other it had felt significant. I feel like an arse thinking that now, especially when I know what I know, but it was how I'd felt at the time. I'd given myself over to her and trusted her; it was the closest I had ever come to real intimacy, unlike the casual times with Aoife back in Dublin. And Holly was softer this time too, beautiful and tender in her movement. But she was also vulnerable, just as I was. I'd watched her the whole time, only closing my eyes when I came. That night something felt different and I began to think that maybe somewhere in our warped connection something good might have started. But then I'd found the notebook and that changed everything.

We went for dinner at Denzel and Alice's and I'd felt strangely relaxed there. If I'm honest I really liked what I saw of my father in the privacy of his own home. As I watched him with Alice, Bill's words came back to me and I could feel myself softening. And then I'd gone to the bathroom via their bedroom. I don't know why. I suppose I wanted an opportunity to get to know him better. That was when I spotted the notebook. It was jutting out, gaping at me and almost begging me to take it. So how could I not? Before I could control myself it was inside my jacket. But there was another reason I went thieving that night. The chances were I would eventually be caught – he would miss the notebook and put two and two together – and a part of me wanted to get caught and for Denzel Anderson to realise who I am.

I hadn't stayed with Holly that night as I wanted to get home and read my stolen property. I took the notebook out and felt its cover, excited to open it but also a little wary. Mammy had been forever telling me that no good came of eavesdroppers, but I had taken the notebook already, so of course I'd read it. It was thin, as if a lot of the pages had been ripped out, and I wondered what had been on them that the writer wanted them removed. When

I opened it I was surprised by the neatness of the writing; somehow I had expected it to be untidy and erratic. The next shock was the writing itself. It was easy to understand, at times quite poetic, and a lot of what I read I could relate to – a struggle with feelings of darkness and black moods, a lot like what I've been feeling since Mammy died. The notebook was filled with thoughts of death and suicide; thoughts about fathers and wishing that there could be a connection; thoughts about a mother's suicide and how to live with it. The parallels between our lives were uncannily close. And then the last surprise came, the one that hit me hardest. It seems that my father is in love with Holly, the girl he met in Ibiza, the girl he claims to have loved from the first moment he saw her, the most beautiful girl he ever laid eyes on. He wrote about what he'd like to do to her and described every inch of her body, a description that could only be written by someone who had intimate knowledge of her. The book is filled with page after page of professions and obsessions until it ends halfway down a page. The rotten truth began to dawn on me.

Denzel's in love with Holly. It makes sense because I felt the tension between them since that first night in the club, but I never dreamt it was anything more than an attraction. I begin to remember the times I'd seen my father go to Holly's alone and things start to look a whole lot clearer. They're having an affair! My rotten father, who raped Marie Sheehan, is deceiving his pregnant wife. Poor Alice! It's obvious that she dislikes Holly – she probably has her suspicions – but she seems to think the world of her husband. Once she finds out about Holly and once I tell her about my mother everything will change. Sure, it will hurt too, but she deserves to know the truth and I will tell her.

And as for the spoilt girl I rightly disliked from the first moment – she and Denzel Anderson are cut from the same rotten cloth. I see that clearly now. All that bull she told me about not sleeping around. Dirty bitch! It seems I came here to make them face up to their wrongdoings, to make them pay. Firstly, my father will get what's coming to him with this powder I have in my hand. Then I will tell Alice everything. Secondly, I will hit Holly in the place where it'll hurt most. Before I leave I'll tell her what I think of her. I'll deface every painting I find in her flat. She'll know that I have the measure of her every time she looks at the pictures she has spent her time in London creating, my own personal contribution to her 'work'.

Denzel is waiting for me outside Rain Dogs and smiles his big smile.

'You're punctual, ja!'

'How could I be late for Depeche Mode!' I say.

'Are you a distant relative of mine or something?' Denzel jokes.

His words just about stop my heart and I'm thankful I was born with a face that's fairly expressionless and unreadable. I shrug.

'Ah'm a bit surprised you like them, given that you're just a pup.'

'Of course! They're legends!'

He waits for me to say more but when I don't he gestures towards the door and we go inside. I'm a bit disappointed with the venue. It seems a bit too big but my dissatisfaction eases as we make our way to the good seats.

'Thanks Clive!' Denzel says. 'He always gets the best seats in the house.'

'So why is he not here tonight?' I ask.

'Family commitments,' he replies, 'the only thing that could keep him away.'

'Well, I guess it was my good fortune.'

'Ja. Can Ah get you a drink?' he asks.

'No,' I say. 'I brought my own gear.' I wait for his reaction.

His face darkens. 'What are you packing?' he asks.

'Cocaine,' I reply and he purses his lips.

'You crazy little fucker bringing that in here!' He sounds really angry now.

'It's fine. No one stopped me, did they? They never do.'

'You use?'

'Yes, but only recreationally. I'm not a junkie or anything!'

'Ja! If you've mastered that art you're one of the few Ah've met,' he says, sneering.

'Yeah, I manage. I just have a little bit every now and then. There's nothing like it!'

I watch my father take in these words and digest them. His expression changes again as if a siren has just gone off in his head.

'But I suppose you know that from your time in Ibiza. I'm sorry, I shouldn't have mentioned it. I'll go sort myself out and see you later,' I say and prepare to leave.

'You be careful, ja?'

'Don't worry about me. I know what I'm doing!'

I leave him, disappointed that he didn't take the bait, but I know it's only a matter of time before he falls off the wagon. He's an ex-junkie; I'd watched enough of them in Dublin to know that the poison always wins out in the end. I go to the toilet and check on the powder still in my pocket. It had been a risk bringing it in here, but a part of me had hoped we'd be caught because then Alice would have her suspicions awakened. Your husband is an ex-cocaine addict and just happens to be caught trying to smuggle it into a concert. Yes, it would have been worth getting arrested. We had been lucky but now perhaps Denzel Anderson's luck is about to run out. I'd seen something flash across his face when I made the proposition. It told me that his addiction is still buried deep inside him and it gave me some hope for a good outcome tonight.

When I go back to our seats I find him just where I'd left him, beer in hand but looking quite agitated. I let a smile settle on my face. Not wanting to ruin the illusion with a poor performance, I decide to say nothing and let my father's imagination do the rest. I swear I can almost feel his anxiety growing as the lights go down and the music begins. This is pure power and I relish the hell he is in, retribution for what he has done to my family. As this dark music crawls up around us I think about Marie. This had been her music too. As we sit there I imagine her dead spirit, as black as the stage in front of me, circling around us as we listen, pushing me to destroy this monster beside me, the person who'd changed the course of her life. I've been thinking so much about her recently, more than I ever did before. Death has altered everything and now she is becoming something else in my memory. I feel sorry for her, and keep imagining how bad she must have felt if dying seemed like an easier option than living.

I'd thought about killing myself for a time after Mammy died. It felt like I had nothing to live for, that her death had taken the best part of me – the part that was directly connected to her. It hurt more than anything I've ever felt before and I thought that death would make the pain go away. They say time flies when you're having fun. I can't remember if that's true. But I can tell you it sure seems to stretch out forever when you're in pain. If I were going to kill myself I know exactly how I'd do it, and now I realise that Bernie never mentioned how Marie had killed herself. I have a feeling it would have been an overdose, like she did before. Me, I would hang myself. But I won't, of course. Marie was one thing, but me? I'm different. I'm made of the same strong stuff as Paddy Sheehan, like Mammy always said.

Dave Gahan sings about getting higher and I applaud his choice of song. It's as if he's a party to what I'm doing. It's just a matter of time before Denzel Anderson slips back into his old habit and then I'll tell him everything. I wonder if he'll plead with me, beg me not to tell Alice, as I am sure Marie begged him to stop all those years ago. Power over another person is a seductive thing and right now, as I allow the blackest part of me to come to the surface to avenge my blood mother's life and death, I feel it and come to understand something that leaves me cold. What I am feeling now, this is the very same energy that made him do what he did. It lives in me too. The notion sends a wave of pure hatred through me, destroying any remaining sentimentality that might have lingered.

I lean towards him when the band are between songs and tell him that I'm going to top up and invite him to come. He doesn't move for what seems like the longest time, but then he turns slowly towards me. His face is fierce. I can feel the adrenaline course through me.

'Okay,' he says eventually, and I feel my heart race as I make my way outside the auditorium, my father dragging himself behind me. In a short time, he will lose everything.

But just as we are looking for a concealed place, his phone rings and stops him instantly in his tracks. He talks for only a few minutes, then ends the call and announces that he has to go. He disappears before I can fully process what has happened. It seems that the gods have changed sides. But it doesn't matter now because I know that I have awakened the urge in him. He had been so close to going back and he'll know this and have to live with it. *When all is said and done you are not so strong, Denzel Anderson.*

I return to my seat and watch the remainder of the concert, and although my father does not come back to join me, the feeling of victory stays with me. It is bitter sweet.

25

Fixing Pia

Marco is dead. Just like that.

Pia is in an awful state, despite everything he did to her. It makes me wonder about human nature and what it is about women that makes them love a bastard. Up until recently I would have proclaimed strongly that I was no such woman, but I find myself thinking more and more about Adam who is, among other things, proving to be quite the bastard. And it seems it is his bad treatment of me that makes me want him more. I have found and got pregnant by a man who is just like my father.

Denzel left us as soon as we got the news of Marco's death and hurried back to his Alice. If there was ever a streak of bastard in Denzel it has disappeared to be replaced by a loyal, loving husband. But maybe that is just while his new life unfolds. Perhaps things will be different once the baby is born and Alice loses her newness. I wonder if she has any idea that her husband has just played a part in having someone murdered. I suspect not. I wonder if this news would drive her away or make her feel more inclined towards him, craving the bad boy and the danger that comes as part of the package.

I go to check on Pia. She is sleeping soundly and looks more relaxed and peaceful than I have seen her look for quite some time. Denzel suggested I should send her back to her parents in Madrid and I think that is the best idea. What do I know about helping someone else get clean? I kicked my own cocaine habit but I was never in Pia's league. Denzel is talking from experience and I should listen to him. And, of course, I have my own situation to think about.

Tonight I will see Adam at Rain Dogs. He has not contacted me since the dinner at Denzel's and his absence makes me crave him more. I know he was with Denzel at the Depeche Mode concert when I called him to come to our rescue. Part of me hoped that Adam would come too but he didn't, and Denzel hadn't mentioned him, but of course we had other problems on our minds. Now the big problem is gone. Dead. I still cannot believe this strange turn of events in my life.

Pia wakes up and looks at me.

'*Bonjour*,' I say, letting my hand rest on her arm.

She doesn't reply.

'I'll make us some breakfast,' I tell her.

'I'm not hungry, Holly – at least not for food.'

'I'll make some coffee then. Come join me,' I say before leaving.

She eventually does, looking awful – even worse than yesterday – and I wonder again if I should take her to a hospital. But I remember what Denzel said: there is no time for hospital. The best I can do for Pia is put her on a plane back to her parents as soon as possible. I hand over her passport, which appeared in my letter box this morning.

'Did they bring any of my luggage?' she asks.

I shake my head. But I am quite shocked by her response. Does she think it was a courier service that Denzel had employed?

'Pia, I think you should go back to Madrid – to your parents – for a while – you know, to straighten yourself out,' I say.

She begins to cry. 'Has it come to this, Holly. What has happened to me! I never thought I would end up like this!'

I pat her arm as if she is a child. 'At least it has got to this point and you can turn it around now. You are lucky. Those men could have killed you.'

She nods. 'I wish they had.'

'Don't say that, Pia.'

'But it's true. I've made such a mess of it. And despite everything I am sorry that Marco is gone. I loved him, Holly. I know he was mean, but there was also a good side to him. He was trying hard to be good.'

'I think you have to straighten yourself out.'

She smiles at me. 'You don't believe I could love Marco,' she says. 'Why does nobody believe this? I saw a different Marco to all of you. He loved me.'

'But he also put you in danger. I do believe you loved him. And I am sorry that you feel bad but I am not sorry he is gone. I am glad, because you are finally free.'

'I don't think I will ever be free.'

'Well, I really believe you will be. So now you should go back to your parents and let them help you to get clean.'

I hand her my phone.

'You are done with me once again,' she says soulfully.

'Call them,' I say, ignoring the accusation in her tone.

She dials the number and I wait until I hear her speaking to her mother before I leave her and go into the studio. I sit and look at the series of paintings that is growing into one of the largest I have ever done and it still feels unfinished. The pictures scare me a little, as I still have this feeling like they are not mine. It is as if someone else came in and painted them, and although Papa has said that this is a good thing, right now it is unnerving. Pia joins me.

'*Mon Dieu!*' she says. 'These pictures are incredible. When did you start painting like this?'

'Since I came to London.'

'You have grown, my friend. I am jealous. I haven't painted in a long time.'

'Well, that is something that you can change very quickly,' I tell her. My phone, still in her hand, begins to ring and she answers it – it seems to take her forever. I understand from her side of the conversation that her mother has booked her a flight today. The call ends and I tell her I'll get her some fresh clothes.

'Holly, will you take me to the airport?' she asks.

'Of course, Pia. Everything will get better from here on,' I say. 'In a few months this will all seem like a bad nightmare. Just you wait and see.'

As we make our way to the airport by taxi, I am conscious that my friend is shaking, probably withdrawing, and I am happy that I can be with her. I feel protective of her now and want her to be safe. I really believe that things can get better. In fact, they have started to get better already and I hope she can see this, despite her despair. We travel mostly in silence and I catch hold of her hand as her agitation grows.

At the airport, Pia checks in and we find a coffee shop to sit in while we wait.

'I hate airports,' she says when we are seated.

'Yes?'

'Too much happening all at once.'

'That is the precise reason why I like them so much,' I reply. 'So you like what I'm doing work wise?' I ask, wanting to get her talking about painting again.

'Yes. It is very biblical. Have you found religion?'

'*Non*. But maybe it has found me. You should start painting again.'

'Have you seen the state of me?' She holds her shaking hands out in front of me. 'I could not even hold a brush right now.'

'I mean when you're out the other side.'

She looks at me and raises her eyebrows.

'You will do it, Pia. Denzel did it and you saw what Denzel was like in Ibiza.'

'But Denzel is stronger than me. I am very weak, Holly. That is why I have ended up like this.'

'No, I won't hear it. It is not true. You forget I knew you from before when you were one of the strongest people around. I was so in awe of you then and that person is still inside of you. She is still there or you would never have come looking for me.'

'You live in a fairytale. But of course your life is good.'

'You know nothing about my life now,' I say defensively.

'And whose fault is that?' she snaps back.

'It only looks hopeless for now,' I say, ignoring her attack. 'You are down and you will be down for a little bit longer, but then you will climb back up.'

'But there is nothing to live for. Have you seen the state of everything? And it is just getting worse. This world we live in stinks. I hate it.'

'I don't believe you mean that. But if we have the same conversation in a few months time I will be more convinced.'

'A few months? You think I will still be around then?'

'Yes, I do,' I reply, determined to ignore her self-pity. 'I think that even in a few weeks the world will look very different. Your parents will look after you and get you the help you need. Denzel moved here to be with his father and joined a recovery group and now he is unrecognisable.'

'But it can all change tomorrow. Marco was sure Denzel would come looking for him, after what happened.'

Pia starts to cry, and I think for a minute that she is going to mention Sid but she doesn't. Of course, while I was falling for Sid in Ibiza my friend was falling away from me, so the significance of it all may have passed her by. I look at her, desperately trying to see that old friend, that strong girl, and to feel some hint of our old connection, but I cannot. She returns my gaze without speaking and then leans in towards me and begins to kiss me. It is a desperate kiss and feels all wrong. I push her away as gently as I can.

'No, Pia,' I whisper.

Her eyes open wide and settle on me coldly. 'Why did you end what we had in Paris?' she asks me and the bitterness in her voice takes me by surprise.

'We both decided we would be friends, and we have been the best of friends.'

'I loved you, Holly, maybe more than anyone else, and you broke my heart. Like you do everyone's.'

Her words fall on me like they have a physical weight and knock every bit of confidence out of me. I want to tell her that it is not true but I do not dare; instead I say nothing. Eventually Pia brings her attention back to our surroundings and tells me once again how much she hates airports.

But her hurtful words linger. She had got her message across to me, the true version of what had happened between us. I had ended our affair, moved on, and she had come with me because she was another Raphael, in love with me but never my friend. I have no real friends, just a collection of people who want to love me. And somehow I have become very good at holding them in place, treating them like things and taking what I need, just like my father.

The realisation that I am just like him hits me with full force and stays with me as I watch Pia walk through the barriers after our half-hearted goodbyes, absent of promises for the future. She had found me here in London and I had paid off an old debt, making up for the heartbreak I had caused her. Now we are done. I watch until she disappears from view. It is no surprise that she does not turn back, not even once, but still it hurts.

26

The Show

I get to Rain Dogs late and Adam is already on stage. I am thankful that he is here. Part of me had been worried that he would not show and I might never see him again. Pia's words had stayed with me, haunting me as I travelled back from the airport. And now I am hoping that I can change the habit of a lifetime and really love someone, really be with someone, as a friend and lover. Perhaps it can be different with Adam.

Pia will be back in Madrid by now. There had been delays on the underground that meant it had probably taken me longer to get across London than it had taken her to fly home. There was so much I could have said back at the airport but I had stayed silent, just listening to her but not reacting. That was the time to speak up and salvage our connection, but I hadn't because she was right, and if I had apologised I would have been admitting to my ill deeds and I could not take her criticism on board at the time. The crazy thing is that the friendship has slipped away, maybe for good, and I am still not altogether sure why I did not speak up when I could have. What is it inside of me that makes it so hard to admit to my bad behaviour? Yes, I am stubborn, but this feels like more than just plain, old stubbornness. Now, safely away from other people's scrutiny, I let myself remember.

Pia was the first female artist I had met and I was really taken with her. I loved her work and was in awe of her freedom. I always believed myself to be a true bohemian, like my papa, but in comparison to Pia I was controlled and tight. Her real name was Gabriella, but she asked people to call her Pia, her artist name. Before that I had never contemplated being called anything other than the name I was given. This alone I found incredibly attractive.

In addition, Pia was very promiscuous and I envied her this sexual freedom. It was every bit as extreme as her art. Up until then there had only been Raphael. Ari and I had kissed but nothing more. After his death Raphael had taken my virginity at my request, and as I floated through art school he stepped in and out of my life. When he met Pia he guessed that our relationship was something more than friendship, even before I did, and accused me of being in love with Pia, an idea I found ludicrous. The truth was that up until then I had never thought about being with a woman, or even that it was a possibility. I have always been attracted to men and, although Pia was very beautiful, the idea of being with her was laughable.

I told Pia about my conversation with Raphael, expecting her to scoff at his accusation, just as I had, but instead she kissed me, proving that Raphael had most certainly read the situation correctly. We had sex and I had enjoyed it very much. My friend was wild and passionate; it felt like I was doing something forbidden. I suppose I am a product of my upbringing and, while Papa is very open-minded, Bebe is quite conventional. Pia told me that I was not her first. She had been with a woman once before and she had found it just as arousing as being with a man, so she could only conclude that she was bisexual. It was not so clear-cut for me, I told her. I did not like labels then, no more than I like them now.

We had continued to be sexual partners for the remainder of our first year at art school, although to be honest I don't altogether know the timeframe involved. It was easy; first we shared accommodation, then we shared a bed. It meant there was always a spare room for Pia's continuous stream of friends arriving at our doorstep. And although I know that I enjoyed the time we were together, for me it was the friendship that meant more. Our affair had eventually ended when Pierre arrived. We had gone to a jazz club where he was playing and he had spoken to us between sets and then after the concert. Pia had been angry that night, accusing me of flirting, and we had rowed fiercely. Her possessiveness had pushed me away and I headed straight for Pierre. My face reddens as I remember how I kept bringing him back to our flat, forcing Pia to watch and assuring her that we were friends, the best of friends. But I had known the truth and I had liked that she had loved me, just as I liked having the same hold I had over Raphael. Now I have lost them both.

In danger of getting too emotional, I bring my attention back to the room and allow myself to be seduced by Adam's mesmerising music. He looks really at home on stage, like he belongs, and the crowd is eating out of his hand. I watch him; if he is aware of me I cannot tell. He seems to perform as if the audience is not here, but the intensity of what he is doing is seductive, as if he is pulling his surroundings into his internal world. I remember when I had first sketched him with his guitar, but tonight I see something more. I am not sure if he is different or if it is because he is performing for a roomful of people, but the connection with his instrument seems to have grown. They have become one, almost as if he is an extension of the guitar. It is the same feeling I get when I have a brush in my hand. The energy seems to come from it to me rather than the other way round. It is not a feeling I am used to seeing in someone else and I wonder if this is because I have had sex with this boy and formed a link.

'Hi, Holly. You okay?' Denzel asks, putting a stop to my thoughts.

'*Oui*, Pia went back to Madrid today.'

'That is the best news, for sure.' He squeezes my arm. 'He's really good. Ja!' he says, gesturing towards Adam.

Adam finishes his instrumental and the crowd bursts into applause. He looks out at us as if he is just noticing us for the first time and I am struck by how beautiful he looks. It is as if he himself is glowing rather than being lit up by the stage light. He shuts his eyes once again and the room falls silent. The audience under his spell, just like me. When he begins to speak I am surprised by his eloquence. Even his voice sounds different as he tells us that he is a huge fan of Tom Waits, that it is a great pleasure to be playing a club that is named after one of the man's best albums; it is only fitting, he says, that he should finish with a tribute. When he begins to sing the hairs on the back of my neck stand to attention. His voice is beautiful. Crystal clear. It makes me want to get lost in it, to allow it to swallow me whole. I am hypnotised by it and, judging by the silence, so are most of the other people in the room. The audience is captivated for the entire song, and when he finishes the applause is even louder than before. There is a cry for more, but he tells us he is done in a voice that lets us know he means it. Now he sounds more like the Adam I know and the magic is broken. At least, for me.

'What was that song?' I ask Denzel.

'It's called "Diamonds and Gold". One of ma favourites actually. Ah have blundered ma way through it a few times but never like that. Ja, the boy has a voice. It's a shame we didn't hear more of it, but maybe next time. So, Pia is in Madrid, safe and unsound,' he says and smiles. 'It's the best place for her.'

'I know. I think maybe our friendship is over.'

'Ja?'

I nod. 'It feels like we're done.'

'Shame. Ah mean she came looking for you when she needed a friend, which should tell you something. Things might look different when she cleans herself up. You think she will?'

'I think it is possible. If *you* can do it, then it is possible, *oui*?'

'Ja, for sure! It's funny how every time Ah come close to toppling, something prevents me. Sometimes Ah think it might be Sid.'

'Your guardian angel.'

'Ja, exactly. Do you use now?'

'*Mon Dieu, non.* That is all behind me.'

'And what about Adam?'

'I have never seen him use. Why do you ask?'

'When we went to see Depeche Mode last night he was packing.'

'How do you mean? He was using cocaine?'

'Ja! It was weird. And the truth is Ah was tempted.'

'But you didn't!'

'Na. But Ah was close, and if you hadn't called Ah don't know what might have happened. Ah suppose the point is Ah didn't. But fuck, you can't take your eye off the ball, ever.'

'You have so much to lose now,' I say, worried for him and angry at Adam. Why would he do that, especially as he had heard Denzel speak about his old habit at dinner? It is also a bit odd as I have never seen him use before. But I suppose I still know little about this boy. None of us do.

'What are you thinking?' Denzel asks.

'Just that I am glad you stayed clean,' I reply. 'Is Alice here?'

'Ja!' He gestures to the left and I see her sitting at a corner table with Bill and Tim. 'She's not too good at the minute. The last stages of pregnancy are tough. She has to be careful. It hasn't been the easiest of pregnancies and she needs to rest a lot.'

'I'm sorry. She's due soon?'

'Ja, she's in her last month.'

'Then everything will be changed!'

'Ja, for sure!'

'Does she know anything about Marco?'

He shakes his head. 'Ah'll tell her after the baby is born and she is back to normal.'

'From what I hear, it is nothing like normal ever again after a baby arrives,' I say and he smiles.

'Ja! Well, Ah'll have to wait and see.'

'You don't keep any secrets from Alice,' I say.

'Not if Ah can help it. Ah want the girl to trust me. Do you know Adam very well?'

'No.'

'Do you trust him?'

'I am not sure yet,' I reply.

'Well, Ah wish you all the best. Both of you.'

'Thanks, Denzel.'

'You want a drink?'

'An orange juice would be nice.'

'You're on the dry again!'

'Yes, for a little bit.' Probably for the next couple of years if this little being inside me keeps on going.

Denzel goes to the bar and, shortly afterwards, Adam joins me. It feels awkward.

'You were incredible, Adam,' I say, not only because I want to break the tension but because I really mean it.

'I didn't see you arrive,' he says and his voice sounds cold, as if he is angry with me.

'I am sorry I didn't get here earlier. I had to take a friend to the airport. It was a bit of an emergency.'

'Fine, whatever,' he replies, sounding like an angry adolescent.

We sit in silence for a bit, and then Denzel approaches with my drink, bringing one for Adam too.

'Boet, you were great! Everyone really loved it!'

'Thanks.' Adam's face reddens.

'That's ma favourite Tom Waits song you sang there.'

'Yeah. Mine too.'

'Ja, Ah learned the guitar riff and Ah would sing along but Ah never sounded like that. You've got a great voice!'

I nod in agreement. Clive calls Denzel over and he leaves us. The silence descends again.

'How have you been?' I ask.

'Okay. Busking a lot.'

I nod.

'What a surprise, Adam Sheehan!' Clive says and joins us at the table. 'You have a super voice. Have you ever covered any Bowie stuff?'

He shakes his head.

'I think you should consider it, especially his early stuff. You'd be great.'

'Yeah, I will.'

'So will you come back next week and do another set?'

'I won't be here then,' he replies and my heart sinks. He is leaving and all of a sudden I do not want him to go.

'You're heading to Dublin for a while?' Clive asks.

He nods.

'Well you should play here again whenever you come back to London. Keep in touch,' he says and hands Adam a card. 'Actually have you ever been to Berlin?'

'No,' Adam answers.

'I was there last week. It's amazing. I know I'm probably cutting off my nose to spite my face as you're good and we need good musicians in this city, but if I were you I'd get out to Berlin. It's a really happening scene and they'd love you.'

'Yeah, thanks. I'll consider it.'

'You really should, mate. How are you doing, Holly?' Clive asks me.

'Yes, I am well,' I tell him.

'Did you know that the boy was so good?'

I shake my head.

'He's a dark horse,' Clive says and his eyes stay on Adam, who reddens. 'Right I should get back to my official duties.'

'You don't like compliments,' I say.

He shrugs. 'I never really know how to react.'

'Just saying thanks is good. My papa says it is the best response and he has a lot of experience.'

'How about you?' he asks.

'I am the same as you.'

'No you're not,' he snaps, and now he sounds really angry.

I ask him if I've done something to offend him, but he is so aggressive that I decide to let it go, and we fall into silence again.

'You're leaving,' I say eventually, trying to sound as casual as possible.

He nods.

'When?'

'Tomorrow.'

'For how long?'

'I don't know.'

I yawn and realise I need to get out of there as I will be dropping off to sleep in no time. One thing I have noticed about pregnancy is that when I get tired, I get exhausted and have to sleep immediately.

'I need to go,' I say. 'Will you come home with me?'

'Not right now,' he replies and my heart sinks.

'But I'll come round later if that's okay. Will you take my rucksack? I've all my gear with me.'

I would be angry if I were not so upset. This adds insult to injury; his dismissal of me hit me hard enough. He cares so little about me that he would let me leave on my own and ask me to take his heavy rucksack with me.

'Yes,' I say, in spite of myself. A different Holly would have told him no way! But I do not want to be alone tonight. I have no one – no Raphael, no Pia, no Sid. So I do something that makes me detest myself while I do it: I give him my apartment keys after checking that I have the spare set hooked to a silver chain round my neck; I tend to be quite careless with keys.

'I will be asleep when you come round, so let yourself in.'

He takes the keys and stuffs them into his pocket and I put on my coat, waiting for him to react to my leaving, but he doesn't.

'I will see you later then,' I say, feeling awkward.

I lift his rucksack, which is even heavier than I anticipated. I struggle to put it on my back as he watches with cold, dead eyes, and then I leave, fleeing before the tears begin to fall and not stopping to say goodbye to anyone.

27

Adam's Eyes: Part V

I see her arrive from the stage and immediately I am angry. I can feel the charge come into the music I am playing – pure raw aggression. Denzel finds his way to her and my rage grows. They talk, sharing their intimate secret, and I am astounded by their brazenness when all the while Alice sits just across the room – lovely, pregnant Alice who was so nice to me tonight when I arrived. Poor Alice, who reminds me so much of poor, dead Marie. My emotions are all over the shop and it pours into the music. But the crazy thing is that this audience seem to be loving it. This is the first time I have performed in front of so many people and it feels like I have been doing it all my life. I had been nervous, but then I was astonished by how great it felt to be on stage. Our good relationship had started at the sound check and has been getting stronger since. Somehow, I feel made to do this.

When I finish, I get the same level of applause that followed every tune and it humbles me more than I ever thought such an experience would. I am grateful to these people for listening to me and I am struck by the great privilege it is to be on a stage. The next thing that happens takes me completely by surprise. I begin to talk and I almost don't recognise my own voice as it tells the audience that I will perform a Tom Waits song. Singing is something I hadn't planned on doing tonight, but it seems that the energy in the room has other ideas. And then just like that, as if I was possessed by someone else, I am singing. It's my first time singing for anyone other than Bernie and Aidan, my two greatest fans in Ireland – my *only* two fans in the world – and I think of them both now, and of Marie, and the emotions flood me. I sing my way through the song and it takes all of me. At the end the audience erupts and I know I am done, that there is nothing else inside me to give, so despite their demands I finish.

As I am packing up, I think about what I have to do next. It would be so easy to walk away but I can't. I will stay and tell Alice what she needs to know. I like her too much to leave her in the dark. Bill is sitting with her like a protective bodyguard and I think about what he said about hurting her. But he doesn't know what I know, and when he finds out about Denzel's affair, I think he will understand why I have to tell her everything. Anyway, I'm off to Dublin tomorrow, so if he feels compelled to punish me for my actions he'll need to come too.

But first I have unfinished business. I walk over to Holly's table and manage to keep my cool, despite the fact that Denzel is holding her arm. Everything is so obvious now and I can feel the charge between them. It makes me wonder how I could have missed it before. I am angry, but I am also hurt. However, I will need to focus on the former energy if I want to see this night through and do what I have come here to do.

They both compliment me and then Denzel goes to get us drinks, leaving me alone with Holly. Thankfully, Clive comes and starts talking about David Bowie and Berlin. I usually find him annoying, but tonight I am glad of the extra company as it means I don't have to speak to Holly. When he leaves us again I can't bring myself to look at Holly, so I keep my attention fixed firmly on Alice and what is going on at her table. Bill and Tim look like they are getting ready to leave, which will give me my chance. Holly begins to talk to me about not being able to take a compliment, and then she has the nerve to tell me that I am like her. I don't fucking think so!

'What's wrong, Adam? Have I done something?' she asks.

'I don't know, have you?' I say, sounding angrier than I would have liked.

She looks at me with no hint of the guilt she should be feeling. Unbelievable! Then she asks me when I'm leaving for Dublin. I keep my answers short and eventually she says she is going home and gives me her keys.

I take them without a word, not wanting to ease her awkwardness. When she is just about to go I ask her to take my rucksack and her eyes fill with tears, which affects me even though I wish it wouldn't. I watch as she struggles with my heavy bag, reminding myself that she deserves this bad treatment. But the truth is, it is hard for me to see her like this so I turn my back on her and make my way over to Alice's table. A part of me is expecting her to come after me, dump my bag and demand her keys back, but she doesn't.

'Adam! Your voice!' Alice says and gestures for me to sit on the empty seat beside her. 'Who would have thought!'

'Yes, wonderful,' Bill agrees.

I blush and Tim Harris looks at me, his expression suggesting that he might know something of my awkwardness. I'm unsure about how to react to these compliments about my music.

'Right,' says Tim, 'we should go.' Both he and an anxious looking Bill prepare to leave us.

'Where's Holly?' Bill asks me, looking me dead in the eye.

'She's gone home,' I reply.

'You take care, Adam,' he says, not taking his eyes off me.

They set off through the crowd towards the exit.

'I was so amazed by your performance,' Alice says, once we are alone. 'And the baby liked it too. He was moving and kicking all the time.'

'It's a boy?' I ask.

She nods and smiles.

'Nice.' A half-brother, I think to myself.

'Yes, and not long now before I get to meet him.' She touches her stomach tenderly.

I tell myself that what I'm doing is best for the baby too. He deserves to know the truth. Just like I did, though it was denied to me until it was too late.

'Alice,' I say, and the seriousness of my tone brings her back to me.

'Yes, Adam,' she replies.

I look at her face, so much like Marie's yet different, softer because it hasn't been twisted by bitterness. And then I feel the full weight of what I am about to do and I realise I can't tell her. I don't want to cause that kind of suffering. That would make me just like Denzel Anderson and I am not like him.

'You look a lot like my mother,' I say

She catches hold of my hand and squeezes it. 'I am so sorry.'

I nod.

'We're calling our baby Sid, after Denzel's younger brother. Has he ever spoken to you about him?'

I shake my head and wonder where she is going with this.

'His mother killed herself too. That was Tim's first wife. You know about Sid surely? Holly must have told you. She and Sid were together.'

My mind begins to work through this new information and I realise what has happened. The notebook. The boy who's mother had killed herself. The boy who had met a girl called Holly and loved her was Sid, my dead uncle, not my father. I had jumped to the wrong conclusion! I think about how badly I had treated Holly tonight and feel awful.

'God, you didn't know! I'm sorry, Adam. I probably shouldn't have told you.'

'No, I'm glad you did. Really. You have no idea ...'

She looks at me confused. 'What's going on Adam?'

'Sorry I need to go now.'

She nods, letting her question remain unanswered.

'Take care of yourself,' she says and gives me a hug.

'Say goodbye to Denzel from me,' I say and leave.

I run all the way to Holly's apartment and wrestle with the key in the lock. My hands are shaking badly, so it takes me a lot longer than it should. Once inside, I look for her in the bedroom but she is not there. I look everywhere and there is no sign of her until there is only one door I haven't opened yet – the studio. I open it, now feeling a little bit like I am intruding. The room is dark, so I switch on the light and I am confronted with an image of myself. It stops me dead in my tracks and everything else leaves me – my search for Holly, my need to put things right, my anxiety about what I've done. The canvas is a mixture of vibrant and vivid greens that capture me instantly, willing my eyes to look deeply so that the picture can reveal itself fully. I am sitting cross-legged and clutching a green sphere, which somehow seems to be three-dimensional, as if I could take it from my painted hands. My face looks troubled and my eyes are lowered, watching the sphere as if it holds the answers to everything. I am completely shocked that all the hours I sat in this room created something so beautiful. I had no idea that Holly was so talented.

Curiosity takes me to the next canvas. I see a man and woman in battle and I get a slow, cold chill down my spine. As I move from picture to picture a story unfolds that is remarkably like my own and I wonder if she knows, if she had somehow guessed. But how could she? Is it possible that she has picked all of this up as she painted me, as if something spiritual had been at work? The pictures look biblical, holy even. My heart begins to race and I get a strong urge to be anywhere other than here, but I cannot move from the spot. I close my eyes, blocking out the external world, and seek some kind of refuge inside. My mind races through a thousand thoughts, taking me back to Dublin, to Mammy and the times we sat together, both struggling to come to terms with the situation. All the precious memories that she had remembered and passed on before she left this world. And yet she had not told me what I was sure to find out: Marie Sheehan's story, the story of how I came to be. I think now about how it would have been if she had explained it to me and saved me finding out from Marie as I had. I wonder if that would have softened the news and made it easier to live with; Mammy was always able to make me feel good about everything.

It's all so obvious to me now – those early years, the conversations and the questions that were left unanswered, the inevitable holes that develop when real events are jumbled up so that a new story can be told, new stories that better serve everyone. I can understand why they never told me the truth. But how can you allow a baby to be born out of such circumstances? And how do I live with this? Marie couldn't. She had killed herself, just like Sid's mother. Sid. My uncle. The man who had loved Holly. Now I realise why she had been drawn to me. Her behaviour makes much more sense. She is grieving, and I am grieving too. Maybe that's what brought us together rather than my need for revenge.

I came to London to find a monster and avenge him. That is where my brain went in its quest to get over the nightmare of knowing what I know. But the truth is, I hadn't found a monster, just a man, someone who did wrong and somehow got on with his life, like I guess we all have to in the face of our worst crimes. I am not a judge nor a jury. The truth is, I am simply someone desperate to belong, just like everyone else.

The door opens and slams shut again quickly. It is pointless to move so I wait to be discovered. Eventually, the artist whose work has just stunned me appears in front of me.

'I can explain,' I say and only then do I notice the notebook in her hand. It seems I am not the only one who has gone in search of things that are not my business.

'Can you explain to me why you took this from Denzel's home?' she asks, looking angrier than I have ever seen her look before.

I prepare to tell her everything.

28

The Notebook

'I can explain,' he says and I wait for the words that will give me clarity.

I had not come straight home from Rain Dogs but instead had sat on a bench close by, crying and worn out from carrying his heavy rucksack. That was when I discovered Sid's blue book, which Denzel had offered me when I went to his house for dinner my first night in London. I hadn't gone searching for it; I had caught sight of it in the side pocket when the street light shone through the folds of material and illuminated the striking colour. The only explanation was that Adam had taken it from Denzel's apartment when we went for dinner. But why?

'I thought it belonged to my father,' Adam says.

'I don't understand! Your father? But this belonged to Sid and you took it from Denzel's apartment.'

He nods, and slowly I digest his words.

'*Mon Dieu*! Denzel is your father?'

He nods.

'But how?' I say.

'My mother came to London when she was a teenager and met Denzel.'

'So us meeting was not a coincidence?' I say angrily, as all the facts start to come together.

He shakes his head.

'What are you doing here? I mean, what do you hope to achieve? Am I part of some twisted game you are playing?' My anger now turns to rage and my voice grows louder. He stands staring at me but offers me nothing, so I lunge at him and push him towards the door.

'Get out!'

He catches hold of me and I am lost in his strong grip; I am no match for this strong boy. Eventually I stop struggling and simply repeat my demand that he leave.

'No, Holly. I want to tell you the truth. Everything. Please. I'm sorry.'

I shrug, not really knowing if I am interested in the truth. I am tempted to run away and hide from all of this.

'Please, can I explain?' he asks, and his voice is like a small child's, which pulls at my heart strings.

'Go ahead,' I say.

'Earlier this year, the person I loved most of all in this world died of cancer as I watched, powerless to do anything to stop it. Afterwards, I discovered that this person, who I believed to be my mother, was actually my grandmother, and my mother, the woman who'd actually given birth to me, was my "sister", Marie. She'd come to London when she was a teenager and met Denzel Anderson at a party one night and he raped her. When she returned to Dublin her mother told her there was no option – she had to have the baby, but she'd not need to raise it. I was born and my grandmother made out that I was *her* child. So Marie had to watch while I grew up. I always knew she hated my guts but I didn't know why. Of course, it all made sense once I found out the truth. I was a constant reminder of the worst thing that had ever happened to her. I decided to come to London to find my father, not to be reconciled but to make him pay in some way for what had happened, for what he'd done. The first day I saw him I was about to approach him when Alice came to join him and it threw me totally. You see, she looks a lot like my mother – well, how she used to look, and I saw she was pregnant. So I stayed back, but I began following him and that led me to you.'

He stops, waiting for me to say something, but I have no words.

'You made everything easy that first day, Holly, when you spoke to me in the coffee shop. You were my way in.'

Now I want to scream at him, to say 'fuck you' and tell him that I hate him for using me. But I stay silent, clenching my fists as if that can in some way help me to keep my mouth shut until he gets to the end of his story.

'But when I met him, I really wanted to believe that what my mother said was a lie, that she said it for the benefit of her parents rather than because it was true. You see, I really liked Denzel, in spite of everything. And my grandfather. And I really liked the idea of having a father and a grandfather. I'd never had that before. I took the notebook because I wanted to discover more about my father. I read it believing it was Denzel's. It's all about how much he loves you and wants to be with you and I jumped to the conclusion that you and Denzel were together. I was disgusted that you and Denzel could do that. I mean, poor Alice! That's why I was so awful to you tonight. I'm sorry!'

I begin to understand and a wave of emotion floods me as I think of what Sid might have written about me to make Adam so mad.

'My mother always said that eavesdroppers never hear good of themselves and she was right. I'm sorry I ever took that bloody book.'

'So how did you discover your mistake?' I ask.

'Alice filled me in about Sid and you tonight and told me that his mother killed herself. It all made sense from what I had read. I had planned to tell Alice everything but I couldn't go through with it, even before I knew the truth. You see, Alice looks so like my mother, but a happier version. And I couldn't take that away from her. And as for you – I didn't even like you at first. But now somehow I like you, maybe even love you.'

'Well, don't look so surprised,' I say and this makes him smile. 'But how can you say that when you treated me so badly? How you were tonight, for God's sake. Making me carry your heavy bag ...' I stop as news of my pregnancy nearly bursts out of my mouth. Now the story has just got more complicated.

'I'm sorry, but I was angry. And hurt. And I didn't know how to deal with it.'

'So you were the asshole!'

'I'm sorry, Holly!' Adam stares at me for a moment. 'Why do you never talk about Sid?'

'To you?' I say with more scorn in my voice than I intended.

'We actually have a lot in common you and I,' he says and despite my anger I am heartened by his statement and what it might imply.

'I came here to forget about him,' I say.

'You came to his homeland to forget about him?' He smiles and I do too.

'Not too bright!' I say.

'You loved him?' he asks.

'Yes,' I reply. 'Very much.'

'How did he die?'

'He found Denzel in some trouble on the beach and tried to help. One of the men attacked him, slit his throat and he died in Denzel's arms.'

'Jesus Christ! I'm sorry!'

'Yes. Me too. It was a waste. It was only afterwards that Denzel discovered Sid was his brother.'

'He's been through a lot too.'

'Yes.'

'I'm sorry I made things so difficult for you.'

'I do not know how to react! I am not used to you saying such things to me.'

'I've been awful to you,' Adam says. 'Sorry! Really! The past year in my screwed up life has left me not knowing what to think of myself. I thought it was the worst thing imaginable, to watch someone I loved so much die of cancer. But when I discovered the other stuff – it was all a bit much.'

'I can imagine,' I say. 'But it doesn't need to mean anything. You know that, yes?'

He doesn't say anything.

'You know who you are. *Oui*?'

'But I don't, Holly, and that's the problem. It's why I had to meet my father – to see the kind of man he is, and discover the kind of man I might be.'

'You can see it like that, or you can see it another way. You were raised by good people. *Oui*?'

'My grandmother was great. Yes. I never met my father –my grandfather, I mean. He died when my sister was pregnant. My grandmother told me she was pregnant at the funeral but the truth was it was Marie that was carrying me in her belly.'

The tenderness with which he says this makes me think about the baby in my own belly.

'My mother – grandmother – always said my "father" was a great man and that I was a lot like him.'

'You see! And she was the person who raised you, who knew you best of all. And now you call her your grandmother, but she was your mother. *Non*?' Now I think of Bebe, my aunt but my mother.

He nods.

'I think you are not an asshole, but a very lovely person if you allow yourself to be,' I say and he smiles, a smile that reaches his eyes and which remind me so much of Sid's. Then I begin to understand why. Sid would be his uncle, after all, and that brings a single question to mind.

'Adam, what age are you?'

He grimaces and I prepare myself for a shock.

'Tell me!'

'Fifteen,' he says eventually.

'*Mon Dieu*! I could be arrested! This is not good.'

'I'll be sixteen before you know it.'

'But you are fifteen now!'

'But in fairness, I have had to grow up very quickly. I don't feel fifteen.'

'And you don't act fifteen, but the fact is you *are* fifteen. Do you know what age I am?' I ask.

He shrugs. 'I really don't care,' he says. He sounds so young and innocent that it makes me want to both kiss him and slap him.

'I am twenty-seven.'

'Jaysus, that's really old,' he says and I laugh. He catches hold of me and pulls me towards him.

'I don't care what age you are,' he whispers into my ear and then begins to kiss my neck.

'Wait! Is there anything else you need to tell me?' I ask and he shakes his head.

'You know everything now. No, wait. There is one more thing …'

I frown.

'I ran away from home.'

'Ahhhh, no more,' I say and he begins to laugh. And so do I, despite the absurdity of the situation.

If there was a time to tell him I am pregnant it is now, when we are speaking the truth, but I don't. I hold back. It is one thing to profess to love an older woman when you are still a child, but quite another to discover that she is carrying your baby. This could tie us together for a very long time.

'Can I ask you a question?' he says when we have stopped laughing. He sounds serious now and I look at him so he knows he has my full attention. 'Has Denzel ever mentioned my mother to you, or what happened?'

'No, but he has been troubled by something, something that he has never found a way to tell me. I wonder if this is the thing he could not talk about when he could so easily tell me so many other things. I think perhaps it is. It would make sense.'

'He told Bill,' he says.

'How do you know that?'

'After I found out Marie was dead I went to Rain Dogs to find Denzel and tell him who I was, but he wasn't there. But Bill was there and he told me he knew already. He'd guessed that I was Denzel's son. He said it was obvious – that I look a lot like him.'

Adam sounds so vulnerable when he says this that I want to reassure him. I run my fingers over his beard.

'Yes, I think if your disguise came off you would look very like him. The jawline, the gap in your teeth. It is obvious.'

'I have to tell him who I am, Holly. I've been talking myself out of it, saying that I should just leave it be, but I have to, don't I?'

'I cannot answer that, Adam,' I say. 'It is your choice.'

'He's my father and he should know, despite how it happened. He is my father.'

'But is he your father, really? I mean he has not had anything to do with your upbringing. Surely that is what really makes a father. Isn't it?'

'Tim Harris didn't have anything to do with Denzel's upbringing.'

'But that is different. Events outside their control brought them together. Denzel met Sid and had no idea they were brothers. Neither of them did. It was only when Sid died that Tim went to Ibiza and Denzel recognised him. It was fated, if that is a word.'

'But maybe it is with me too. I mean, you came and talked to me in the coffee shop.'

'*Non*. With you it is different. You came looking for this situation, Adam. And Tim and Denzel's relationship is different ...'

'You mean Tim didn't rape Denzel's mother.'

'I'm sorry, Adam. I would like to be able to say that it doesn't matter but it does. I don't think Denzel will want anyone to know what he has done. Would you?'

'But it had consequences. Me! I exist and he has to know that. To accept that.'

'But what if he cannot accept that? Can you handle it if he does not?'

He shrugs. 'Maybe my mother said he raped her just because she was too ashamed to admit that she had sex and got pregnant.'

'But Denzel told Bill it was true.'

'Bill said these thing are never clear cut. I mean, they were both very young. They could have have got it wrong. Think about what happened with you and me that first time!'

'Do you honestly believe that?'

'Well, it's possible.'

'Of course, all things are possible. But do you believe that your mother was lying?'

He looks down and shakes his head. 'I'd like to believe it.'

'So what do you want from Denzel? Be honest, Adam. What do you really want?'

Again he shrugs.

'I think there are perhaps two possibilities,' I say. 'You want to make Denzel pay for what he has done, to make him face up to his ill deed. Or you want to have a connection with him.'

'I think I want both.'

'But the question is, which do you want more?'

'I don't understand.'

'To want to make him pay comes from a place of vengeance. But to want to be connected to him comes from a place of, well, love I suppose. And somehow I think your intentions, good or bad, will play out and shape the final outcome.'

'So the consequence of my actions will be governed by whether my intentions are good or bad.'

'Yes, I think so.'

'It makes sense, but the truth is I don't know which it is and I'm not sure I can separate the two.'

'Well then, there is only one way you can know for sure. Tell him and see what happens.'

Adam nods. 'Will you come with me?'

I don't altogether understand why – perhaps it is because I am carrying his baby or maybe it is because he looks at me now like a little boy – but I tell him yes, God help me!

29

Baby Sid

Sid Anderson was born at 7.55 a.m. on Friday 13th November, three weeks early, and weighing 7lbs, the text message tells me as I lie in bed. There is a photo as well of the brand new baby bundle.

'Alice has had her baby,' I say to Adam, and he rolls over and looks at my phone. He takes hold of the handset and scrutinises the picture, only returning it when he has drunk his fill completely.

'Do you want children, Adam?' The question just slips out.

He shrugs. 'Do you?'

'Yes,' I reply and I could swear that the baby inside me reacts.

'I want to tell my father who I am. Today!' he says.

'Are you sure? I mean it might not be the best time right now. He will be very emotional.'

'So when would be the right time?'

'Yes, I see your point. But still, it does not have to happen right now.'

'But it feels like it should, before I go back to Dublin.'

The mention of Dublin sends an emotion my way but, surprisingly, it is one of relief.

'And you'll come with me, like you said?' He looks at me with big frightened eyes and I cannot refuse.

'I said I would, didn't I!'

'Thank you!'

'When would you like to go?'

'As soon as we're up and dressed,' he replies.

'I think your timing might not be the best. Seriously.'

'I can't wait any longer, Holly. I just want the truth out there!'

'And what if he reacts badly. What then?' I ask.

'At least he'll know he has another son.'

'But what if he tells you he wants nothing to do with you? Will you handle it?'

'I'll have to, like I've handled everything else.'

'Because you've handled everything else so well!'

'Given the circumstances, I don't think I did too badly.'

'Have you been in touch with your family at all?' I ask.

He shakes his head. 'Not since I heard about Marie.'

'Do you not think they might be worried?'

'Well yeah, but I'll be back there soon enough.'

'But why not call now and tell them you are coming?'

'You're very bossy!'

'And you are very stubborn!'

'I'll call my sister after we see Denzel, okay?'

'Okay.'

We arrive at Rain Dogs in the afternoon and meet Denzel as arranged. He had agreed to the meeting easily, of course, because he has no idea about what it is about. I have a bad feeling about the whole thing but don't say anything to Adam in case I make it worse. Denzel lets us in the side door with a huge grin on his face.

'Congratulations,' I tell him. 'I am surprised you are not at the hospital.'

'The joys of running a club! It's the one day that no one else could be here for a beer delivery so here I am, on the best day of ma life!'

It might be about to become the worst day, I think, wishing Adam had listened to me.

'Hey, Adam,' he says and shakes his hand. 'Wow, Ah wonder if your lekker performance had anything to do with why Alice went into labour last night. Ja! Ah like that idea. Little Sid was so impressed with your music that he thought, Ah want a piece of that world.'

Adam turns red and I begin to feel really uneasy, hoping that he will be unable to go through with this, just like when he had tried to tell Alice.

'So can Ah get you fine people a drink?' he asks.

'I'll take an orange juice,' I say.

'Me too,' Adam pipes in.

'Okay, it's orange juice all round then, although a bottle of fizzy might be more appropriate! But Ah guess it's still a little early in the day. So, last night was fantastic, Adam. How would you feel about a Monday night residency? We could do with acts like you.'

'That'd be great, but I actually wanted to talk to you about something else.'

'Ja?' Denzel looks puzzled.

'I'll wait until you're sitting down,' Adam says.

'You think Ah need to be sitting down?' Denzel laughs, but it is not his usual laugh and it makes me feel really anxious.

He comes and joins us at the table, hands us our drinks and then sits down slowly.

Adam takes Sid's notebook out of his bag and puts it on the table. 'I took this from your place the night we came for dinner,' he says. He sounds nervous and I don't blame him; I watch Denzel's face begin to darken.

'You went snooping around ma house. Why would you do that? Ah don't understand!'

'I thought it belonged to you,' Adam says.

'But why would you take ma stuff. Are you some sort of freak?' he says and laughs nervously.

'I'm your son.'

The words tumble into the room like blocks of ice.

'My mother met you in London sixteen years ago,' Adam says.

Denzel's face drains of all its colour and he begins to chew on his bottom lip. Adam and I wait for him to say something but he doesn't. He keeps his eyes fixed on Adam. I am about to speak when, without warning, Denzel jumps up from his seat knocking the table and the glasses into the air. It makes me scream. He lifts Adam out of his seat and drags him across the room as if he weighs nothing.

'Denzel, please don't do this!' I shriek.

But he does not stop. He kicks the door open and drags Adam out into the street. I am frozen, unable to move until Denzel reappears through the doorway and orders me to stand up.

'What did you do?' I ask, shaking my head.

'Get the fuck out of here, Holly! And don't ever come back – either of you!'

I look at him, speechless. Gone is the charming man of five minutes ago; now it is the wild, dangerous Denzel of Ibiza that presents himself. I remember him well and at close proximity he looks less appealing than he did in my fantasy.

'Did you not hear me?' he shouts, snapping me from my trance.

I go outside and find Adam bent over in a way that makes me think Denzel had punched him in the stomach.

'Are you okay?' I ask and he shakes his head. I put my arms around him and lead him to a nearby bench.

'You were right, Holly,' he says eventually.

'I am sorry,' I say. 'I wish I could have been wrong.'

My arms are wrapped around him and he leans into my chest. For a moment he feels like a baby, even though I am the smaller of the two of us. Somehow he fits perfectly and feels tiny in my arms. I close my eyes and visit my future, imagining the time when I will hold my baby like this. We sit like this for what feels like a long time, me with my not-yet-born child in my mind's eye and Adam seeking what neither his mother nor grandmother can now give him.

After a while my attention is drawn to a window across the road from where Denzel is watching us. He disappears and moments later the door flies open. He bursts outside as if the building is burning and, for a time, I am worried that he might be coming to attack Adam again. But he does not. Instead he walks straight past us as if we do not exist. Just as I had suspected, things could not have gone more badly. I feel for them both really strongly and I wonder if this new empathetic version of me is down to the new life inside me.

I remain motionless, seeing Adam as I have not seen him before, waiting patiently for his cue to leave. As I hold onto Sid's nephew, I wonder what would have happened had Sid been here and the Harris family were hearing this news; I would have met Adam in a completely different way. But there is no Sid any more; there is only this boy holding on to me. I have been here for him in his darkest hour and I am glad of that. But to think that there might be a future for us together is ludicrous. The idea of me ending up with Sid's nephew seems kind of hideous. Yet I am carrying his child. I am pregnant, carrying Denzel Anderson's grandchild, Tim Harris's great-grandchild. What a strange turn of events!

Adam and I walk the short distance back to the apartment, but today it takes longer for some reason. We stroll along at a snail's pace, not talking, as usual, but today there is something new in our silence – it is less uncomfortable. With every step I take, my future becomes clearer. There will be no union between Adam and me. He will go back to his family in Dublin and I will go back to mine in Paris. I know it in my bones as sure as I know that nightfall is on its way. I have been here for this significant thing in his life. I have paid for the new life he has given me and will repay my debt when I let him go, free to grow up into a man who may eventually have a family. But right now he is a child himself and to blame him for what has happened would not be fair. This is my gift to him, just as the life growing inside me was his gift to me. As we walk along I think that perhaps I do love this boy, and I believe what Papa said about love: it is freedom. Maybe what I have been doing with this love that is 'for the birds' is not love at all but something else. The realisation makes me feel more prepared for the little person inside me who will require my love above everything else.

I feel an inner warmth and then Adam squeezes my hand. It makes me wonder if he might have felt it too.

30
Adam's Eyes: Part VI

As soon as we get inside the apartment I begin to kiss her, desperate to become lost in what is happening now so that I can forget what has just happened elsewhere. We undress each other on our way to her room and by the time we fall on to her bed I am already inside her, feeling it as intensely as before. It makes my toes curl. I come and I think she does too, although I'm not altogether sure and I don't have the courage to ask.

Afterwards we lie side by side, and I find her hand and hold it. We breathe in unison, fast to slow, saying nothing, just lying and enjoying the feelings that have been ignited. My breathing begins to quicken again, one of my body's less obvious ways of telling me I want her again, so I roll on top of her and this time we make love for a long, long time. We roll from position to position, and all the time I manage to stay inside her; it's as if we have been practising this all our lives. I feel as close to her as I have ever felt to anyone. All the other stuff falls away. Right now, none of it is important.

I hadn't come looking for this, but it had found me. Perhaps this is the real reason I came to London – to meet this girl. I feel a lot for her. I told her I thought I loved her but she hadn't said it back, maybe an indication that she is the adult here after all. But love is a huge word, a loaded word, one not to be used lightly. Love is something that needs to be invested in; that's what Mammy used to say. It seems weird to be thinking about Mammy as I lie with this naked girl. I wonder what she would think of Holly. I think she'd like her, but the age gap would come as a shock. Of course, it's pointless to be thinking about this as Mammy will never get to have her say.

Holly falls asleep in my arms and I hold her tightly, stroking the side of her face. 'Thank you,' I whisper into her ear, hoping that some part of her hears me. She had been so lovely to me after my father threw me out of his club. She was kind and I didn't expect that, and I'll never forget. As I think about it now it makes me ashamed about how badly I'd treated her before. I'd underestimated this girl and I'm sorry. But hopefully a little of how I have been with her in the past few hours will make it better between us. Holly's sleep deepens and she turns away from me. This is when I should turn and lean into her but I don't. Instead, I roll off the bed and slip on my t-shirt, not sure where I'm going and what I will do until I get to her studio door.

The paintings are just as striking as before and this time I look at all of them, even the ones that are hidden from view. I get lost in them and don't notice her come in until she speaks.

'I should sue you,' she says.

'I'm sorry! I couldn't help myself. I love your work, Holly. And, well, I'm involved.'

She nods.

'Did you paint Sid?'

'Yes.'

'And I reminded you of him and that's why you approached me in the coffee shop.'

She nods. My attention moves back to the pictures. 'Do you realise that this is kind of my story you have painted?' I ask.

'Yes.'

'But you didn't know it. It's a bit frightening how it appeared here on the canvas.'

'Not frightening, I think. Mysterious. Magical. When I paint I feel like life moves through me.'

'I think I know what you mean. It's how I felt in the club when I played.'

'Yes, I saw it. You are a musician, Adam, just like your grandfather. It is a gift. And now you must make sure that you spend your life cultivating it.'

'I don't think I'll have a choice,' I say and she smiles a knowing smile.

'You are the artist and that is why you were born. You carry the gift that came to you from Tim Harris.'

'That is the nicest thing anyone has ever said to me,' I tell her and bring my hand up to touch her face. 'You are beautiful, Holly, when it counts and where it counts.'

She doesn't say anything but her eyes tell me she heard.

'I'm cold,' she says eventually and breaks the spell. 'Let's go back to bed.'

And so we do.

In bed, I ask the question that is at the front of my mind. 'What happens now?'

'You will go back to Dublin to your family. And I will go back to Paris to mine.'

'You don't think that we should stay in contact?'

'No, Adam, I don't. I think we were meant to come together for this moment, but now it is time to move on.'

I nod because I understand. 'You still love Sid.'

'Yes,' she says. 'Very much. And you being his nephew, well, I am in danger of hooking on to you for all the wrong reasons.'

'But I don't mind. Hook on to me all you want,' I say and she smiles.

'You say that now, Adam, but you will mind and you will resent me for it in time. You are just starting out and there are many girls for you to meet. Then there will be The One. And when you meet her you will know it with every fibre of your being. I cannot explain it to you. Words are not enough. But you will know what I mean when you meet her.'

'But maybe I've met her now.'

'If you had there would be no talk of *maybes*. I promise you this.'

'That is how it was for you and Sid?'

'Yes,' she says. 'It was very special.'

'I'm sorry he died, Holly,' I say eventually.

'Thank you, Adam,' she says and we fall into silence.

I hold her in my arms and she drifts off to sleep again quickly. I watch her and wonder if her head is filled with memories of my dead uncle. I feel intensely for her but what she's said makes sense. Our attachment to each other was born out of loss and the need to clutch on to something – someone. It would be easy to hold on to each other but it would never be right. We don't belong together. Of course we don't! To stay together would keep us stuck in this piece of our stories that needs to become a part of our histories.

I remember her kindness from earlier, exactly what I needed after my father lost it with me when I had revealed our connection. His reaction told me that Marie Sheehan had been telling the truth: he *had* raped her. The ending to our story was inevitable. He had pushed one son back out of his life on the day that another, my half-brother, had come to stay. I remember the picture I saw on Holly's phone, the one that had set this latest chain of events in motion. After I saw my little brother I knew I had to tell Denzel. If there was a possibility that I might be a part of his family and that little baby's life, I had to know. And I thought it was possible, I really had. But now, as I sit watching the beautiful artist sleep beside me, I can clearly see the impossibility of it. I mean, how do you explain something like this to your wife and child? It would be pointless to stay in Denzel Anderson's life because he does not want me here. And the truth is, if I were in his position, I wouldn't want me here either.

But it is his sin to deal with, not mine. I did nothing wrong. I was born. That is the significant thing. Now I know the truth and his rejection hasn't killed me. I'm still here. And I've learned that I'm an artist; a gift I got from this family lives inside me, and now I see things differently. Maybe a picture or a piece of music can save a life! I have a feeling that music might just be about to save mine. I had felt the charge of being on stage enough to know that I'll go back there. Perhaps that is where I belong.

Holly shifts, leaning into me, and I hold her for a little while, just long enough for her to fall into a deeper sleep. Then I gently roll her over and let her go. I watch her breathing in and out. It is comforting. How easy it would be to stay! I close my eyes, blocking her from view, and slide out of bed. I get dressed in the dark and, grabbing hold of my rucksack, I walk quietly towards the bedroom door without looking back. Something tells me that even if she wakes up she won't try to stop me. I close the door behind me.

The view over Tower Bridge draws me towards it one last time and, as I watch its light reflect in the Thames, I think about everything that has happened to me in London: meeting my father and grandfather; meeting Holly; playing at Rain Dogs; my confession; making love earlier; and now leaving. I could never have foreseen any of it and yet something tells me that it had happened just as it was meant to. I'm not sure how long I stand there, but whatever it was that held me suddenly lets go and I make my way towards the front door.

Holly's phone lies on the messy coffee table. I pick it up, find her number and tap it into my phone – a direct line of contact should I need it. And then I call her and save my number on her phone, the first entry in her contacts and impossible to miss. I take a last look at the picture of my baby brother, the brother I will never know, wishing him all the luck in the world and set the phone down.

I take the first step through her doorway, out of her life and my father's life. Then I just keep going, one step at a time, until I am back on a bus heading for the boat that will take me to Dublin. In my mind I imagine a video playing backwards, taking me back through the steps that had got me here in the first place. But, of course, I am moving forwards; backwards is never an option in this life. If it were, I wonder would I choose to do things differently. I had come to London with a heart full of hate, or so I thought, but yet when I met my maker, my father, it was not hate I felt. Far from it. Meeting him – and Holly – has been significant. But now life goes on. I hadn't come from the best of starts but that didn't mean it couldn't change; it didn't mean I couldn't be a 'good' man, like Mammy always said I could be. The bus rolls me forward and Mammy's memory whispers to me. She tells me that everything will be just fine.

'Wake up, mate, we're here!'

The voice belongs to the coach driver and pulls me out of a deep sleep.

'Thanks,' I say and smile at him.

He smiles back, his huge face almost bursting at the seams and I wonder what has made him so happy.

'Take care of yourself, mate.' He says it like he really means it, and I tell him I will.

On the boat I find a quiet corner and take out my guitar and begin playing. The music wraps itself around me, making a thousand promises. Today there is a new freedom to my playing, so much so that my journey goes by unnoticed, and I slip out of England and back into Irish shores in what seems like the blink of an eye.

Back in the city centre, I feel light and at ease, like a person who has just set down a heavy load. I fall into the rhythm of Dublin's streets again and take comfort in the Irish accents that pass to the left and right of me.

The taxi appears out of nowhere and there is no time to react. I take the full impact. Everything slows right down as I am thrown upwards. It feels like I'm flying through the air for a long time with no real idea of when I will land. I just know that when I do, it'll really hurt.

31

Crossed Lines

As soon as I wake up, I remember he is gone. I had heard him leave as I floated between sleep and wakefulness, but I chose to sleep. It was easier for us both to just let him go without goodbyes.

I get up and have my breakfast, all the time aware of what is growing in my belly. I feel heavy in the mornings, like I could have a second sleep, and I believe this is down to the mini life form on board. It is an extraordinary thing, when I think about it, that I have the beginnings of what will be another person inside me. How wonderful life is! As I think about the baby I fantasise about how it would be if Sid were here with me and it was our baby inside of me. And yet I feel as if it has all happened as it was meant to. It couldn't have been any other way. There was a baby to be born and Adam and I did that, but it was my connection to Sid that made it happen. After he died I sometimes wished he had left me pregnant so that I had a piece of him still here with me, and now it feels like I have, for Harris blood will run through my baby's veins. Yet none of this really matters for either way the fact remains the same, I will have a baby, a child that will be loved and will have the best start. Papa, Bebe and I will see to that. I wonder again how my papa will take the news when I return to Paris with a series of paintings and a new life in my belly. He will need to be the 'father figure' while Adam Sheehan grows up to become the man he believes he is right now.

Once in the studio I look at the paintings, filled with the boy who has left my life as suddenly as he appeared. They make me wonder if we simply become what is mapped out for us in the womb; as my baby is knitting together inside of me is the person he or she will become being set now? Or are we made up mostly of the experiences we collect as we live? I do not have the answers now, but I will be watchful of this new life in order to find out. Imagine! I will get to see this child from the beginning all the way to its grown-up version. Made by Adam and me.

My phone rings in the other room and as I am in no rush to answer it it goes to voicemail. I am just about to return to the studio when it begins to ring again. This time I make it.

'Holly.'

'Denzel?' I say, the shock registering in my voice.

'Can we talk?'

'Of course,' I reply.

'Ah'll come to you, ja?'

'Okay.'

A short time later, a serious-looking Denzel arrives at my door. We do not hug, I suppose it would feel all wrong considering how we last parted company.

'Coffee?' I offer and he nods.

He joins me as I make the first jug of the day. These days not only is the smell unappealing but the little one seems to object by giving it a vicious aftertaste if I drink it, so I don't bother. However, I cope with the bad smell as I am glad to have something to occupy me, otherwise the tension in the room would be too much. Denzel's unease is both apparent and uncomfortable.

'Ah'm sorry, Holly,' he says, and I turn around and hand him his hot coffee.

'Yes, so you should apologise. You were mean. But it was understandable. Apology accepted.'

'How long have you known?' he asks when we eventually sit down.

'Just a day before you. I found Sid's notebook in Adam's bag, confronted Adam and he told me.'

'What did he tell you?'

'That he only found out about you earlier this year when his grandmother died. Up until then he had believed she was his mother and that his biological mother was his sister. After he found out he was angry, so he came here to find you – to make you pay.'

Denzel's face reddens. 'Ah raped his mother.'

'He was not sure if it was true. He thought that maybe she lied. But I think you showed him she was telling the truth.'

'Fuck! I can't believe it! Do you remember when Ah was in Paris and Ah went all funny at your exhibition?'

I nod.

'Your picture made me remember. Ah'd honestly forgotten – imagine that! And it was the worst thing to remember. Or at least Ah thought it was! But to realise that Ah made her pregnant. Ah don't know what to do with this, Holly!'

'Do you need to do anything with it?'

'Ah need to tell Alice and Ah will lose her. Ah deserve to lose her. Today Ah was watching her with baby Sid and Ah felt like the unluckiest bastard ever to walk the planet. Ah mean, ma life is how Ah dreamt it could be. Ah'm so happy. But Ah don't deserve her! Ah don't deserve to be happy!'

'That is absurd, Denzel. We all do bad things!'

'Na, some people don't – people like Alice.'

'I refuse to believe that she has not done a single bad deed! But if you are so worried, don't tell her. Adam is gone. He has let go. And you should too.'

'Ah can't keep this from her. Ah have another child. Sid has a half-brother. How can Ah keep something like that to maself considering ma own story!'

'But this is not about you and Sid, Denzel.'

'Na, it's about Adam. Ah can't keep this to maself. Ah used to dream Ah had a son. Ah actually felt that ma flesh and blood was walking on this planet. And he was! But never in ma worst nightmares would Ah've dreamt it would be how it is! It's a fucking shambles.'

He looks as if he will cry and I attempt to put my arms around him, but he pushes me away.

'Na, Ah don't deserve any sympathy, Holly! Ah made this mess. The carousel ride is over and it's time for me to get off, back to how ma life was always meant to be. Ah thought Ah'd finally come good, that despite all the wrong turns Ah could put maself back on the right road, but it's not true. Ah fucked it all up a long time ago and there's no going back. Ah should never have contacted Alice again!'

'*Mon Dieu*, Denzel! It is not true. You have a family – the most important thing. If you feel so strongly about it, then tell Alice. If she really loves you, which I think she does, she will love you still and see past this. And if she doesn't see past it then you should make her. Fight for her, for your family!'

He says nothing for a long time.

'Ah had a feeling in the pit of ma stomach that something like this was coming,' he says eventually. 'Ill deeds come to swallow us up in the end. The point is, you can run from them and you can spend your life forgetting, but there is a wheel that is turning and it always comes full circle. For sure. You know Ah left Alice pregnant when we were fifteen?'

'No, Denzel, I didn't!' I am jolted by this new information, considering my situation with Adam.

'Ja, Ah got her pregnant and left because Ah was afraid. She had the baby, but he died at birth. Yet Adam lived, in spite of the circumstances.'

'Babies are simply born, Denzel. It is we who provide the backstory.'

'It's a shame he found out. It's a lot for a kid to take on. He's what – fifteen? Ja, Ah thought he was older.'

'*Touché*!' I say.

'Ah mean, how do you live with that?'

Tears begin to roll down Denzel's cheeks. This time he lets me put my arms around him and hold him in much the same way as I had held his son the day before.

'Why did he not tell me sooner, Holly?' he asks eventually.

'He planned to when he first got here, but then he saw you with Alice and he couldn't. He tried to tell Alice too. When he read Sid's diary he got some nonsense into his head that you and I were having an affair and he wanted to punish us both.'

'Na!'

'Yes. But he realised his mistake when he discovered he was reading somebody else's words.'

'So someone finally read the blue book!'

I nod.

'Poor kid. Ah remember when Ah came to find ma father, and how it felt to be rejected. Ah swore Ah would never do that if Ah had a child come look for me, but Ah did. It seems we just repeat history all the time, so what's the fucking point?'

'Denzel, you must listen to me! This is really important – for all of us. Don't tell Alice. Adam is gone. He will get on with his own life and you must too. You owe it to baby Sid and Alice. If you tell her you will invite her to share in your nightmare, to spend dark nights wondering what it means, and it will continue to haunt you both and eventually destroy what you have. But you can move on with your family and forget Adam, so that all your lives can be good. And you must forget me.'

'What do you mean, forget you?'

'Our connection is broken. We should both move on too. Sid is gone and I want to forget him now. I am going back to Paris and I think we should forget about each other.'

'But, Holly, Ah don't want to forget about you,' he says.

'Well, I want to forget about you, Denzel. And Sid. And Adam.'

'It's over between you.'

'Of course!' I say. 'He is fifteen, Denzel!'

'Ja, Jesus!' He smiles and I can't help but smile too.

'I pick them well!'

'But he picked you too, na?'

'Yes, but actually I was drawn to him and now I know why. He reminded me of Sid. Everything in my life for the last year has been about Sid and I need to move on or I will go crazy. Papa said that to me and I told him he was wrong but it is true. I just want to leave London and get back to Paris and forget all about this, and I think you should too.'

'But Ah promised Sid Ah'd look out for you …'

'Stop this! Sid is dead! He is gone. And Marco too. Let it go. All of it. Forget so that you can start again. You have a new Sid in your life. *Oui*? A new chance. Do it right this time! Yes?'

My phone rings just as I stop talking, as if it was waiting for me to finish my important speech first. I answer it without thinking. The voice is Irish, with an accent a lot like Adam's, but it is not Adam.

'Hello, are you a relative of Adam Sheehan?' the man asks.

'*Non*,' I reply, 'a friend.'

'I'm afraid there has been an accident, miss.'

'Is he okay?'

Denzel is watching me now like I am some object he might need to catch in the near future.

'It's a bit early to say, miss, but he took a bad fall. He was hit by a taxi. Those fellas drive like crazy, so he's all messed up, but he's still with us, which is the main thing.'

'Where is he?'

'They've taken him to the Mater Hospital.'

'Is that in London?'

'No, miss, you'll need to get yourself to Dublin.'

32
Blood Relatives

I walk the distance from Tower Bridge all the way to the South Bank, saying goodbye to London. Sid had drawn me here and now I am leaving so that I can forget. I want to move on and let go, just like I told Denzel to. I have had enough of living in the past, especially now that I am carrying the future. It is crazy! I arrived here little knowing that I would leave pregnant. But I suppose that is how it works. I walk into the next moment with no idea and it turns itself into what I call my life. My story. And the next part of my story will take me back to Paris.

Adam is fine, some broken bones but nothing that will not fix itself. He was lucky, I was told by the hospital when I called to check. My phone number was in his phone contact list and that was how the Irish policeman contacted me. My number was the last call on his phone – I had spotted his missed call on my phone – and hence the first one they called. Hearing about the accident had been a shock, and I thought about going to Dublin to be with him as I waited to hear how he was. But as the days passed by and the distance grew between us, I knew I would not.

Denzel had left my apartment in a state, not knowing what he would do, although something flashed in his eyes when he heard about Adam that made me think he might not be able to just walk away, to leave it all like I am doing. But I suppose it is not so clear-cut for him; after all, Adam is his son and he can be sentimental about these things. My only wish is that my child will never know any of this mixed-up story. My choice is to walk away from the

Harris–Anderson–Sheehan legacy, and I intend to keep it at a great distance from me and my child.

For the last week I have worked most of the time in between napping. The pregnancy makes me tired and I find I cannot go long stretches without taking rest. But this has been a blessing, as I find that just after sleeping my energies are heightened – or perhaps it has to do with this baby inside me. In addition to working and resting, I have been walking, but only in tiny spurts, not like today's marathon, which is about saying goodbye. My pictures will be shipped back to Paris this afternoon and I will follow them tomorrow. I called Bebe and Papa last night and they are preparing for my homecoming. All three of us will sit down to dinner tomorrow night and I will tell them the great news that I am to be a mother, that there will be another person in our little family. I have a feeling it will be a girl somehow. I dreamt of a little black-haired girl in a green dress, and when I woke up it had felt like I had met my daughter, a mini Holly. She will be blessed with a family who will love her.

This is my new beginning, a chance to get on with my life, leaving the past behind. It is time to forget and put my energy into my future. I am moving forward. My legs feel tired so I take a seat by the Thames, the river I have sat beside a lot during my time here, dreaming and preparing myself to let go. I open up my phone and go to my contacts. Adam's is the first name, an entry he must have made. I delete it, wiping him away. And then I scroll down until I find Denzel's and I do the same. Pia is next to go. I find Raphael's number and my finger lingers, but I push through my reluctance and make him vanish too, respecting his wish to be free of me. Lastly, I go to the name I have kept on my phone even though I know it is pointless. I look at Sid's name, the man I loved more than anyone, then I press delete and say goodbye.

Everything is in order. The last thing to do is to walk back to my papa's apartment and pack up my things. It hits me strongly: a feeling of being totally alone completely overshadows everything else, all my thoughts of new beginnings and futures and babies. I begin to cry, holding nothing back, and it feels good, like I no longer have to stay strong or be immune to my emotions. A stranger comes and joins me on my bench, a man wanting to be my knight in shining armour, but I do not accept the helping hand being offered. No more strangers in my life. I tell him that I am pregnant – he is the first person I have told – he wishes me luck and leaves me at such a speed that it is almost funny. I begin to laugh hysterically and he looks back at me, grateful for having had a lucky escape. I laugh for a long time and it feels like the best medicine. How quickly these moods of mine can change! I take advantage of my mini high and use its energy to walk back home. Much to my surprise there is a little spring in my step despite my tiredness.

When I first see the familiar figure perched outside my front door, I think I must be hallucinating given my recent emotional rollercoaster. However, he does not disappear; instead he grows more vivid.

'You are real!' I shriek and allow myself to fall into his arms. I know he will catch me as he has been doing for most of my life. My dear Raphael has come back for me. I had let him go but he has come back.

He lets me sob, and holds me in much the same way as I had held both Adam and Denzel. Now it is my turn, and I take it with gratitude. I cry until I have no tears left and then we go inside.

'I will make coffee,' Raphael announces.

'Just water for me,' I say.

'Holly Du Plessis refuses a coffee! I have heard it all now!'

No you haven't, sweet friend, I think to myself.

'A lot has happened while you have been away,' I explain. 'But first, tell me why you are here?'

'Jean-Claude,' he replies and I nod.

'He is worried about you. He called in to see me in Milan, asking what all of this was about, me no longer being your friend, and I tried to explain to him but you know your father, he was hearing none of it.'

I smile, remembering my conversation with Papa when he was here.

'He told me that I should not give up on you, Holly, especially if I really love you. He said that if I did I would always regret it and wonder what might have happened.'

'But what about your girl in Milan?'

'It didn't work out. How could it! I thought about you all the time. My grand gesture has put you more in my head than ever. You told me the truth the last time I was here and it was not what I wanted to hear. But Jean-Claude is right – if I give up on you now I will always wonder.'

'But it was not the truth, I think! Papa had one of his conversations with me too while he was here, telling me that this love I speak of is "for the birds", and maybe he is right. Perhaps all of my dreaming and romanticising means that I miss the important feelings that are around me. I have missed you, Raphael, and the truth is that when anything happens in my life it is you that I always want to turn to. And that must mean something. But I see now that how I have been to you is unfair, and you are not the only person I have treated badly. I think I am more like my papa than I like to believe.'

He says nothing, which tells me everything.

'I am sorry for how I have been – behaving like a spoilt child. Perhaps it is time for me to grow up.'

'What are you saying, Holly?'

'I am not sure. I cannot make any promises to you and I would not dare. But I do love you like my family, and I want things to be better between us, to be different. I want you in my life. And now there are no closed doors any more, so maybe what you ask for is possible.'

'That is all I have ever wanted to hear,' he says and smiles at me, pressing my nose with his finger the way he has been doing since the first time we met. He leans in to kiss me but I stop him.

'There is something I have to tell you first, so you know everything. No secrets.'

He nods and settles back, putting space between us again. When I am sure he is listening I begin.

'I am pregnant.'

'Now that is something! The boy who you were painting?' he asks and I nod.

'Do you love him?'

'No.'

'Not like your Sid.'

'I am not even sure about that any more. I think it is easy to say you love what is not here to test you.'

'Does he know – the boy?'

I shake my head. 'Only you and I know.'

'And you will have the baby?'

I nod.

'And you would like me to be involved?'

'I think so.'

'And how would we be?'

'I don't know, Raphael.'

'But how do you think you would like it to be – if it could be any way you wanted?'

'I would like for us to be a family – for you to be the baby's father. And to be my husband.'

'Was that a marriage proposal, Holly Du Plessis?'

'I don't know,' I say honestly, my face reddening.

'If I were to ask you to marry me what would you say?' he asks.

'You would want to marry me even though I am carrying another man's child?'

'But only we know that.'

'It would be your baby, Raphael, as far as I am concerned. You would be her father.'

'It's a girl?'

'I have a feeling.'

He smiles. 'I have always secretly wanted a baby girl. Daddy's girl, you know. Like you and Jean-Claude.'

This makes me cry all over again. 'Yes, like me and Jean-Claude,' I say between sobs.

'So now I will ask you again. Will you marry me, Holly Du Plessis?'

'Yes, Raphael Conti. I will.'

*

'Chérie, merci! Tu es à la maison!'

Bebe, the woman who I have only recently come to know is my blood relative embraces me. But the truth is, it did not matter for I have always thought of her as family. She raised me; she is my mother, just like Raphael will raise our child and we will be his family. This is the bond that ties – the love that is shared with us as we grow, nurturing and preparing us for when we have to do it on our own. The last twenty-four hours have been quite astonishing. Something is very different between Raphael and me. We are as close as we've ever been but there is a tension that has left us, now that all the doors are open. We made love last night and that too had been different.

Tender. And I did not think of Sid. I feel alive and no longer walking with the dead.

Bebe tells me that I look good, that I am glowing. I tell her that I had the best time in London and I am very happy, that Raphael and I have some news and she does not look particularly surprised. She tells me she has missed me so much and she cries. And so do I because I am emotional these days but also because I am flooded with love for her. My mother.

'*Où est Papa*?' I ask and she tells me that he is on his way and will join us for dinner tonight. And I reply that it is perfect as I have something to do today. She asks me if we will be four tonight and I nod, which makes her smile. She is very much on board with Papa's plan, I see!

I leave Bebe and walk through the streets of Paris, getting a feeling of being home again. I walk all the way to my family doctor, Doctor Tarde, and his receptionist tells me I am lucky, that he has a space in an hour so I book in and I leave to wander around Paris some more. As I am sitting by the Seine my phone rings and I know exactly who it will be.

'*Bonjour, chérie*! You are settled back.'

I ask him to join me as we have an appointment to see the doctor in an hour. He tells me that he will be with me in a flash and I hear the happiness in his voice. It comforts me to know that I am the cause of this happiness. But, more than that, it makes me happy too. True to his word Raphael is with me moments later, not a difficult feat since his apartment is across the street from where I am sitting. We remain silent and watch the autumn sun's reflection on the water, as we have done many times before. When it is time we wander hand in hand the short distance to the doctor's surgery.

Doctor Tarde hugs me, shakes hands with Raphael and invites us to sit. He does not ask me why I am there but instead waits for me to tell him. I suppose the presence of Raphael must be a giveaway. I say I am pregnant, and then I look at Raphael and he smiles. Doctor Tarde congratulates us both. It feels significant, as if it in some way affirms our story; the truth will remain our secret, known only to two people. It is a secret that will bind us further together. I know for I can feel the ties forming already as Raphael sits by my side.

Doctor Tarde tells me that pregnancy tests are ninety-nine per cent correct, but just to be completely sure he will take some blood and have it tested. I nod and smile. As he takes my blood he tells me I should get used to being prodded and pulled at, now I am pregnant. He should have the results within a week and he will call me then and let me know. He believes that my father will be thrilled by the news and I agree. Jean-Claude has always been very vocal about his wish for grandchildren. A final congratulations to us both and we are on our way.

Raphael has an appointment, something to do with work, and I tell him that I will go home and rest before dinner. He kisses me with the same tenderness that has developed between us since I told him about the baby. It makes me feel safe and secure.

When he leaves me I go back to the river's edge and sit watching the water, thinking about how good it feels to be back home and ready to get on with my life. Me, Raphael and our baby. Adam Sheehan and Denzel Anderson are gone from my life and it will stay that way.

And then I think about Sid, my beautiful boy from London, and realise that without him none of this would have happened. He has left but the love has not. It continues.

'Thank you,' I say and smile. And just for a moment I let myself believe that he hears me.

33
Adam's Eyes: Part VII

I open my eyes and see Denzel Anderson. At first I think I might be dreaming, but my aches and pains tell me not.

'Ah'm sorry,' he says.

'How did you find out?' I ask, curious to know what got him here.

'A policeman phoned Holly.'

'A guard,' I say.

He looks confused.

'We call them guards here, not policemen. Is she here?'

'Na. She's gone. Ah'm sorry.'

'I can't blame you for that,' I say.

'You can if you like. You can blame me for anything right now.'

'Why are you here?'

'Because you're ma son.'

'Does Alice know?'

' Ja.'

'And Tim?'

'Ja.'

'Do they know everything?'

'Of course.'

'You raped Marie Sheehan.'

'Ja, Ah did. It happened when Ah came to London looking for ma father, Tim Harris. He told me that he didn't want anything to do with me, that he had nothing for me and Ah was about as angry and bitter as it's possible to be. That's when Ah met your mother at a party. We were fooling around and when she told me to stop, Ah flipped out. Ah was high, but it was more than that. Ah kept going because Ah wanted to punish her, to make her feel pain like Ah was feeling. And then Ah left her crying. Ah left feeling like a nasty piece of shit and wanting to forget it'd ever happened.'

'It messed her up, you know,' I say, feeling the need to speak for my dead mother.

He nods and looks away.

'They made her have me and then pretend that I was her brother. She always hated me and I never understood why before. But of course she hated me – I'm the living image of you. Even I can see it.'

'Ja. You're ma boy, for sure. This might sound weird, but Ah always felt like Ah had a son somewhere. But for a different reason. Before Ah came to London, Ah grew up in Cape Town with Alice. We were childhood sweethearts and she fell pregnant. Ah wanted us to run away, but she insisted we tell our parents. Anyways, it didn't work out as we planned. Her father beat me and so did ma stepfather and Ah ran away. But Ah always thought she had our son. And she did, but he died at birth.'

'You ran away from her and she took you back?'

'Ja, she loves me for some reason, for which Ah'm ever thankful.'

'And even now that she knows about me?'

He nods. 'She told me to come and get you. She said that Ah should know you and you should know your little brother.'

'She looks a lot like Marie.'

'That Ah remember. Ah thought about finding your mother to see if she wanted to press charges. But then Ah got another chance with Alice and Ah chickened out. But Ah'd a feeling that it would come out. But not like this, Ah have to say. Na! You were a shock of huge proportions.'

'I don't think she would have pressed charges.'

'Na?'

'I think she'd have been glad you were sorry and that finally someone was acknowledging what happened to her. I don't think anyone ever did.'

'Ah'm sorry about that. Truly Ah am!'

'I believe you,' I say.

'You could've lied to me, you know. If you'd told me that Marie was lying I'd have believed you.'

'Ja, but only the truth will set you free.'

'Do you really believe that?'

'Ah don't know, Adam, but maybe Ah'm about to find about.'

We hear them before we see them, Bernie and Aidan. They've been coming every day, keeping vigil by my bedside since the accident.

'Oh hello,' Bernie says to Denzel, openly curious. 'Are you not going to introduce us to your friend, Adam?'

My father looks at me as sheepishly as I have ever seen anyone look.

'Sure, Bernie,' I reply. 'This is Denzel Anderson, my father.' It doesn't sound wrong at all. On the contrary, it sounds just right.

SID III

I watch as she goes through, startled and seduced at the same time. Once again it feels as if I'm experiencing something unique, a thing for which no words exist. Marie, the woman who I helped in her time of transition, has gone and I am left wondering if I will be here forever. Stuck. Dead, but still in my life between the worlds.

Marie committed suicide, just like my mother, and somehow me sitting with her and listening gave me some closure. Talking to Marie made me feel as if I was finally getting Penny's side of the story. Marie mentioned her mother a lot and as soon as she called her by her full name, Peggy Sheehan, I knew without question that she was the same Peggy that had comforted me when I first crossed over into this place. I was excited because surely this meant I would go soon, just like I had seen Peggy do. The mother had been here for me, I would do the same for her daughter, and then it would be my time. It made sense. Universal order. I guess I was so wrapped up in my story that I didn't see what was obvious and so it was only when she took us to Adam that the full extent of our connection became apparent. Adam links what is left of our families. Peggy must have discovered this when Adam appeared but she chose not to tell me. And now I understand why, as I didn't tell Marie for the exact same reason. My time with Peggy had been about me and she had watched me come to terms with the end of my life. Now it's about Marie and it would not serve her to know.

Marie and I were there through it all, the confrontations and the discoveries, as Adam left and Raphael returned, when the car hit Adam, and Holly took the call just as she was advising Denzel to move on and forget. We watched as Denzel confessed to Alice, knowing that he risked everything, and she told him that the only thing that mattered now was that he put things right. So he told Tim Harris about his other grandson, then made the journey to Dublin and told his son, Adam, the truth. Marie Sheehan and I watched as the two people who she'd blamed her entire life for her awful pain had somehow found comfort in each other's existence. And in that moment she went. She let go, seeing the same thing that her mother had seen as she watched her grandson begin his search for his father. And yet I am still here, watching my brother and his son begin what up until a short time ago seemed like an impossible connection. I have let go of my father, my brother, my life, but there is one love that keeps me here.

I go to her now, back by the water's edge in Paris where she had spent most of her time after I died. I can feel her and see her, but she's oblivious to my presence. She had been able to feel my presence those few times in London, but today all of that is gone. Things are different now. She has returned to Paris to marry Raphael and, as I watch her in the early stages of pregnancy, I am filled with longing and sadness. Why could this not have happened for us? Why had I died before we got a chance? I had been angry when I heard her tell Raphael that she wasn't sure that she ever loved me. *You had loved me, Holly*! And it's not easy to love a dead person any more than it is to love a living person when you are dead.

'Why can't you see me, Holly?' I ask, crouching down and touching her face. But what would be the point of her seeing me. I am gone, dead, and she is alive. She has said goodbye, decided to move on with her life.

I'm sorry that she has let me go. But what do I want? Surely I want her to be happy? And then I realise the real reason why I am still here. It's because I am waiting for her to come and join me. And I realise now why I refuse to let her go. I am afraid that if I do I might never find her again. But she isn't coming any time soon, and I have to stop this.

I take a last look at her face and kiss her lips tenderly. In that kiss I remember how much I love her and I offer it to her, all of it, so that it keeps her safe and well and loved in her life.

'Thank you,' she says and smiles.

And then it happens, the indescribable thing that I'd watch happen first to Peggy and then to Marie, and it is every bit as spectacular as I had imagined.

About The Author

In addition to writing fiction, Kira Kenley is a singer-songwriter and teacher. She lives in London with her musical husband and their lunatic cat.

Her first novel *All The Way Back To Here* was published in 2013. *Awakening Alice* is the sequel; *Adam's Apple* is her third novel and concludes The Harris Trilogy.

To connect with Kira visit www.kirakenley.com

Coming soon ...

Ocean Cry
It shouldn't be possible that somewhere like 'Ocean's Perch' can exist in a world where mostly Nature and her rules are ignored. But it does, for a reason that is shortly to become obvious to everyone on the withering planet Earth, as it fast runs out of resources. And time.

Babylon Taylor, one of the three hundred and thirty-three inhabitants of Earth's last paradise, is the child through which Nature chooses to speak. But will those around her listen and finally understand? Is it possible that humankind can live in harmony, both with each other and with the outside forces that surround them? Babylon believes it is. But now she must convince everyone else.